*Your Duck
Is My Duck*

Your Duck Is My Duck

Is My Duck

STORIES

Deborah Eisenberg

ecco

An Imprint of HarperCollins*Publishers*

Heartfelt and abiding thanks to the Lannan and MacArthur Foundations—and many thanks also to Kimberly Cutter.

HarperCollins books may be purchased for educational, business, or sales promotional use. For information, please e-mail the Special Markets Department at SPsales@harpercollins.com.

FIRST EDITION

Designed by Suet Chong

Illustrations on pages 119, 131, and 143 provided by Shutterstock, Inc.

Library of Congress Cataloging-in-Publication Data has been applied for.

ISBN 978-0-06-268877-4

18 19 20 21 22 LSC 10 9 8 7 6 5 4 3

For David, Lucy, Jenny, Nell, Lev—and, as ever,
of course, Wall

Contents

Acknowledgments

"Your Duck Is My Duck" was published in *Fence*.

"Taj Mahal" was published in *The Paris Review*.

"Cross Off and Move On" and "Recalculating" were published in *The New York Review of Books*.

"The Third Tower" was published in *Ploughshares*.

Your Duck
Is My Duck

Your Duck Is My Duck

Way back—oh, not all that long ago, actually, just a couple of years, but back before I'd gotten a glimpse of the gears and levers and pulleys that dredge the future up from the earth's core to its surface—I was going to a lot of parties.

And at one of these parties there was a couple, Ray and Christa, who hung out with various people I sort of knew, or, anyhow, whose names I knew. We'd never had much of a conversation, just hey there, kind of thing, but I'd seen them at parties over the years and at that particular party they seemed to forget that we weren't actually friends ourselves.

Ray and Christa had a lot of money, a serious quantity, and they were also both very good-looking, so they could live the way they felt like living. Sometimes they split up, and one of them, usually Ray, was with someone else for a while, always a splashy, public business that made their entourage scatter like flummoxed chickens, but inevitably they got back together, and afterward, you couldn't detect a scar.

Ray had a chummy arm around me, and Christa was swaying to the music, which was almost drowned out by the din of voices in the metallic room, and smiling absently in my direction. I was a little taken aback that I was being, I guess, anointed, but it was up to them how well they knew you, and I could only assume that their cordiality meant either that something good had happened to me that was not yet perceptible to me but was already perceptible to them or else that something good was about to happen to me.

So, we were talking, shouting, really, over the noise, and after a bit I realized that what they were saying meant that they now owned my painting *Blue Hill*.

They owned *Blue Hill*? I had given *Blue Hill* to Graham once, in a happy moment, and he must have sold it to them when he up and moved to Barcelona. *Blue Hill* is not a bad painting—in my opinion, it's one of my best—still, the expression that I could feel taking charge of my face came and went without making trouble for anyone, thanks to the fact that, obviously, there were a lot of people in the room for Ray and Christa to be looking at, other than me.

How are you these days, they asked, and at this faint suggestion that they'd been monitoring me, a great wave of childish gratitude and relief washed over me, dissolving my dignity and leaving me stranded in self-pity.

Why did I keep going to these stupid parties? Night after night, parties, parties—was I hoping to meet someone? No one met people in person any longer—you couldn't hear what they were saying. Except for the younger women, who had piercing, high voices and sounded like Donald Duck, from whom they had evidently learned to talk. When had *that* happened? An adaptation? You could certainly hear *them*.

It was getting on my nerves and making me feel old. I'm exhausted, I told Ray and Christa. I can't sleep. I can't take the winter. I'm sick of my day job at Howard's photo studio, but on the other hand, Howard's having some problems—last week there were three of us, and this week there are two, and I'm scared I'm going to be the next to go. And as I told them that I was frightened, that I was sick of the winter and my job, I understood how deeply, deeply sick of the winter and my job, how frightened, I really was.

Yeah, that's terrible, they said. Well, why don't you come stay with us? We're taking off for our beach place on Wednesday. There's plenty of room, and you can paint. We love your work. It's a great place to work, everyone says so, really serene. The light is great, the vistas are great.

I'm having some trouble painting these days, I said, I'm not really, I don't know.

Hey, everyone needs some downtime, they said; you'll be inspired, everyone who visits is inspired. You won't have to deal with anything. There's a cook. You can lie around in the sun and recuperate. You can take donkey rides down into the town, or there are bicycles or the driver. What languages do you speak? Well, it doesn't matter. You won't need to speak any.

Naturally I assumed they'd forget all about their invitation, so I was startled, the day after the party, to get an e-mail from Christa, asking when I could get away. One of their people would deal with the flights. I could stay as long as I liked, she said, and if I wanted to send heavy working materials on ahead, that would be fine. Lots of their guests did that. It could get cool at night, so I should bring something warm, and if I wanted to hike, I should bring boots, because snakes, as I knew, could be an issue, though insects were generally not. I would not need a visa these days, so not to worry about that, and not to worry about Wi-Fi—that was all set up.

I doubted that anybody else who visited them would not know exactly how to prepare, and yet there was Christa, informing me so tactfully of everything, like snakes and visas, that I'd need to know about, by pretending that of course I'd already have thought of those things. A week or so later a messenger brought a plane ticket up the five flights of stairs to my little apartment, which was when it dawned on me that the good thing Ray and Christa had perceived happening to me was that they now owned one of my paintings, which meant, obviously, that it most likely was, or would soon be, worth acquiring.

My job at Howard's studio expired, along with the studio itself, at the end of the following month, just in time to save Howard and me from my quitting right before I got on the plane. At least it was no problem to sublet my apartment, even at a little profit, to a guy who liked cats, because as everyone was observing with wonder, the real estate collapse had not flattened rents one bit.

Howard looked around at all the stuff that represented his last thirty years. Bon voyage, he said. He gave me a little hug.

The plane took off in frosty grime and floated down across water, from which the sun was rising in sheer pink and yellow flounces. It was a different time here—must that not mean that different things were happening? I'd brought my computer, but maybe I could actually just not turn it on, and the dreary growth of little obligations that overran my screen would just disappear; maybe the news, which—like a magic substance in a fairy tale—was producing perpetually increasing awfulness from rock-bottom bad, would just disappear.

I had exuded a sticky coating of dirt during the night on the plane, but in the airport, ceiling fans were gracefully turning and the heat was dry and benign, like a treatment. As everyone exited with their luggage, I kept peering at the e-mail from Christa I'd printed out, which kept saying: *Someone will be waiting to pick you up.* I had her cell number on my phone, I remembered, and scrabbled in my purse for it, but as I pressed and tapped different bits of it and stared at its inert face, I was struck by how complete the difference is between a phone that works and a phone that doesn't work.

For a long time, whenever I traveled anywhere, it had been with Graham, who would have thought to deal with the issue of international phone service, even though Christa hadn't mentioned it. And as I stood there, a lanky apparition ballooned up into the void at my side, frowning, mulling the situation over. Graham! But the apparition tossed back its fair, silky hair, kissed me lightly, and dissipated, leaving me so much more alone than I'd been an instant before.

Wheeling my bulging, creaking suitcase here and there as my mind cluttered up with great, unstable stacks of potential disasters, I located an exchange bureau, and my few sober monochromatic bills were replaced by a thick, fortifying sheaf of festive ones that looked like they were itching to get loose and party. Onward! I thought, and swayed on my feet from fatigue.

I was deciding which exit to march myself to and then do what when Christa strode up. "The driver and Ray got into some big snarl," she said, hustling me along. "And he took off. He's acting out all over the place."

"He's, like, crashing into stuff?" I said.

I wasn't managing my suitcase fast enough to keep up with her, and she grabbed it from me irritably. "He's buying something."

"A car?"

"What? Did you remember to hydrate on the plane? Some subsidiary. It always makes him crazy, but, hey, nerves are a *weakness, I'm* the one who's nervous. So this morning Mr. Sang Froid accuses the driver, who by the way is also one of the gardeners and a general handyman, but what difference does it make if everything falls apart, of scratching the Mercedes, which I happen to be one hundred percent certain is something he himself did the other night when he came home blind drunk at dawn and almost demolished the gate. So the driver stormed off, just before he was supposed to leave to pick you up, and then Ray stormed off, too, in a black cloud, to God knows where. Plus, the place has been crawling with, just who you want to hang out with, accountants. Well, one of them's a lawyer, and I think there's an engineer, too. They look like triplets, or maybe it's quadruplets, hard to tell how many of them there are, you'll see. They're Ray's guys, his pets, a week ago they were golden, guaranteed to go for the throat, now all of a sudden they're a heap of sloths who just lounge around swilling his wine and hogging up his food, which big surprise, and he fucking well better be back for dinner, because *I'm* not entertaining those turnip heads. Don't worry, you'll be okay, though—Amos Voinovich is here, too, except he's pretty antisocial, which I didn't really get until he showed up, and it turns out he hates the beach. He says he's working, which is great of course—maybe he'll do something for us while he's here. And anyhow, he's better than nothing."

"Amos Voinovich the puppeteer?"

"Well, I mean, yeah. You know him?"

I didn't know him, but I'd seen one of his shows, which was about two explorers and their teams. There were puppet penguins and puppet dolphins and puppet dogsleds and of course puppet explorers fighting their way through blizzards and under brilliant, starry skies to be the first to get to the South Pole. Voinovich himself had written the lyrics and the music, which was vaguely operatic, and each explorer sang of his own megalomaniac ambitions, and various dogs from each team sang about doubts, longings, loyalties, resentments, and so on, and the penguins, who knew very well that one explorer's team would prevail and flourish and that the other explorer's team would die, down to the last man, sang a choral commentary, philosophical in nature, that sounded like choirs of drugged angels. The eerie melodies were often submerged, woven through the howling winds.

Christa chucked my suitcase into the trunk of her car, and as we sped up winding roads in the brilliant sunshine, the deluxe night of Amos Voinovich's puppet show wrapped around me, and while Christa groused about Ray, I kept dozing off, which was something I had not been doing much of for a very long time, and her voice was a harsh silver ribbon glinting in the fleecy dark.

We came to an abrupt stop in front of a smallish house,

covered with flowering vines. "This is where you and Amos are. I put you in the same place, because you're the only two here right now and it's easier for the staff. You'll be sharing a kitchen, but I mean nothing else, obviously."

"Accountants?" I asked, stumbling out of the car.

"They're staying in the main house with us, unfortunately. Ray insisted, although we could perfectly well have given them a bungalow. They've got their own wing, at least, across the courtyard. You'll see them at dinner, but except for that you won't have to deal with them. I gather they're all taking off tomorrow."

She brought me into the little house, which was divided in two, except, as she'd said, for a kitchen downstairs, which both Amos and I had a door opening onto and which appeared to be very well equipped, though meals and snacks and coffee and so on would always be available in the main house. She showed me light switches, and temperature control for my part of the house, and where extra blankets and towels were kept. Dinner was early, she said, at eight, and no one dressed, except once in a while, if someone happened to be around. Lunch was at one. And breakfast was improvisatory. The cook would be on hand from six, because sometimes Ray liked to swim early. Did I have any questions?

I gaped. "Guess not," I said. "Um, should I . . . ?"

"Yeah, come on over whenever you want," she said, and gave me a quick, squeamish hug. "So, welcome."

What was not dressing? I was incredibly tired, despite the little nap in the car, but not even slightly sleepy. I opted for jeans, which were mostly what I'd brought, and when the clock on the night table informed me that it was 7:45, I went over to what I assumed was the main house and wandered through empty rooms until I happened upon Christa, who was wearing a little vintage sundress, the color of excellent butter.

Dinner meant helping yourself from a selection of possibilities including some things on platters over little flame arrangements and then sitting down at a long, polished table that probably seated thirty. Amos the puppeteer did not in fact show, but the accountants or accountants plus lawyer plus engineer were there. They didn't wear jackets, but they all wore exhaustingly playful ties, which suggested, I suppose, that Ray's forthcoming acquisition was so sound that chest-thumping frivolity was in order. Ray had reappeared, and said hello to me, but barely, giving me a bitter little smile as though he and I were petty thugs who had just been flagged down by a state trooper, and that was the last notice of me he took that evening.

I watched, through the glass wall, as evening slowly began to rise in the bowl of the valley below and soft lights glimmered on. Up over the mountains, though, it was still day. A dramatic terrain. The soft, mauve twilight currents were rising around the table, so you didn't really have to converse, or you could sort of pretend that you were conversing with someone else. Somewhere in that gently swirling dusk the accountants were talking among themselves—telling jokes, it seemed. Their bursts of raucous laughter sounded like reams of paper being shredded, and after each burst they would instantly sober up and swivel deferentially around to Ray.

Terrain—was that what I meant? "What language are they speaking?" I whispered to Christa, who was sitting in a darkening cloud of her own.

"You really better drink some water," she said. "Don't worry, it's all bottled. There are cases over at your place, by the way, I forgot to show you, in one of the cupboards, but tap is okay for your teeth."

It was English, I realized, but specialized. One of them was finishing up a joke that seemed to concern a Pilgrim, a turkey, a squaw, and something called credit swap rates.

They all laughed raucously again. Ray was drumming his fingers on the table, making a sound of distant thunder. The accountants et cetera swiveled around to him again with sweet, boy's faces, and he stood up abruptly.

"Gentlemen," he said, with a tiny bow. "I have a great deal to gain from this transaction, assuming it all proceeds as anticipated. But if at zero hour, by some mishap, it should fall through, let me remind you that, owing to the billable-hours clause you were so kind as to append to our contract, only you will be the losers. I salute your efforts. I have the highest hopes, for your sake as well as mine, that your irrepressible confidence in them is justified. But perhaps a moment of sobriety is in order at this point, a moment of reflection about the tenuous nature of careers. Or, to put it another way, don't think for a moment that if the boat is scuttled, I'll throw you my rope. I'm sure you all recall the Zen riddle about the great Zen master, his disciple, and the duck trapped in the bottle?"

He drained his large glass of wine, glug glug glug. "Everyone recall the master's lesson? *It's not my duck, it's not my bottle, it's not my problem?*" He slammed his empty glass down on the table and wheeled out.

"What did I tell you?" Christa said.

What *did* she tell me? I had no idea. Presumably I'd been dozing at the time, soaring aloft on polar winds as the two explorers savagely pursued their pointless goal under the remote, ironically twinkling stars.

"Plus," she said. "I think he's seeing someone here."

"Oh, wow," I said, and I thought of the bite that every morning would be taking out of her beauty and glamour and how rapidly an individual's beauty and glamour could be rendered irrelevant by standards that had been embryonic only months before, or supplanted by some girl who was just about to walk through the door. "Oh, wow," I said again.

"You can say *that* again," she said. The accountants et cetera had disappeared from the table, I realized. All that was left in their place were crumbs.

"Well, so, good night, I guess," I said, as she wandered off. "Guess I'll just be going back over to the, to the . . ."

Upstairs in my bedroom, I began to unpack, but there was the issue of putting things wherever, so I decided I would leave all that until morning. I set up my laptop after all, though, as tossing out my old life seemed both less plausible and maybe less desirable than it had some hours earlier.

I fished my pj's out of my suitcase and opened the shuttered windows for the breeze. I was listing, as though I were drunk, which I supposed I was, from all the wine it had seemed appropriate to toss down at dinner, but mainly I was exhausted, though still wide awake, as I was so often—wide awake and thinking about things I couldn't do anything about. Couldn't do anything about. Couldn't do anything about. Also, an unfamiliar, somewhat rhythmic tapping suggested that there might be a beast, some brash snake, for example, in the vines just outside my window, trying to get me to open the screen and let it in.

To account for my snoozing in the car, I had mentioned to Christa my exasperating resistance to sleep, and just before we sat down at the table she gave me a few pills, wrapped in a Kleenex. "What are they?" I'd asked. "They're Ray's," she said. "He won't notice."

A few months back, I'd gone to a doctor about sleeping problems, and he'd asked me if I wanted pills.

"I'm afraid they'll blunt my affect," I said. He looked a little disgusted, as if to remind me that he had a downtown practice and I was not the first self-obsessed hysteric he'd dealt with that day. "Then your best bet is to figure out why you're not sleeping," he said.

"What's to figure out?" I said. "I'm hurtling through time, strapped to an explosive device, my life. Plus, it's beginning to look like a photo finish—me first, or the world. It's not so hard to figure out why I'm not sleeping. What I can't figure out is why everybody else is sleeping."

"Everybody else is sleeping because everybody else is taking pills," he said. So I got a prescription from him, and I took the pills for about five nights running and flushed the rest down the toilet. They got me straight to sleep all right, before I'd even had a chance to boot up the worries, and I would sleep for hours and hours, but then I would wake completely exhausted, having spent my night fighting my way through dark tunnels that stank of a charnel house, thwarted everywhere by slimy, pulsing lumps, my own organs, maybe, and in the morning, when I'd get to work painting, I seemed to be sloppier, or less demanding than I'd formerly been. Maybe my painting wasn't any worse than it had been, but I sure didn't mind enough that it wasn't better.

So then, when I stopped taking the pills and it mattered again that my painting wasn't better, I had to wonder *why* it mattered.

I had to face it—my affect was blunted, pills or no pills, unless weariness counted as affect. So, I decided that I'd make myself stop painting for a while, or maybe forever—that I'd stop unless something forced itself on me that I'd dishonor if I didn't paint better than I was able to. And so I did not send materials on ahead to Ray and Christa's, because the trip seemed like an ideal opportunity to clear my mind of whatever impediments to that, and even if I was left with nothing in place of the impediments, at least the sun would be shining.

I heaved my suitcase onto a luggage rack—things had been thought of—to get it out of the way of bugs, even though if there were bugs, I'd probably brought them along in my suitcase, and listed on my feet again. I needed to hydrate, probably, I thought, so I went downstairs and opened the door to the kitchen to search for water.

A bony little person wearing a red and black striped shirt and skinny red and black plaid pants was sitting at the table, regarding me with huge black eyes that looked as though they were rimmed with kohl. He had a lovely, large, downward curving nose, and a face so waxen and intense in its penumbra of black curls that it left an afterimage.

"Am I disturbing you?" he said.

"Not yet," I said. "I mean, we've hardly met."

"The noise?" he said.

Spread out in front of him on the table were scraps of fabric and colored paper and little figures made out of clay and wood and various other materials, a pot of glue, and some tools, including a little hammer—oh.

"Hey, I loved *Terra Nova Dreaming*," I said. "I really did."

"Good," he said. "Because I could use your opinion on this new one. I want to try running it here, but it's gotten pretty out of control—there are a lot of characters, including some bats that have to turn into drone aircraft and back again, which is a pretty tricky maneuver. There are a couple of kids from the village who can help me backstage, and Fred can deal with the lights, but I'd appreciate a good supplementary eye out front."

"Fred?" I said.

"A guy who drives and gardens here and stuff. I don't know what his name really is. That's what Ray and Christa call him. He's good at doing things, but he's a bit erratic, I think. I don't want to take too much of your time, though. Christa told me you were coming, and I figured you wanted to get your own stuff done, or why else would you be here."

"Well, I mean, to relax?"

"Yeah? You must have a really unusual relaxation technique going."

I furrowed. "Why do you . . . ?"

"Hey, even some of the world's champ relaxers didn't show this season—haven't you noticed? The whole crowd has bailed—all the other freeloaders and the usual apparatchiks . . . I'm here because I got evicted from my apartment when the arts program at the school where I was teaching got cut, and what with putting the new show together and not exactly having an income, luxury handouts were definitely attractive, whatever the hidden costs. I figured you were coming for some similar reason. Anyhow, the onus is on us, obviously."

"The onus . . . ?"

"The onus? To entertain, to distract, to diffuse, to buffer? On us, as in on you and me? Which is why I hardly ever put in an appearance at the main house, and, as I established the policy immediately, it's been interpreted as a sign of genius, I hear from Fred, if I understand him correctly. Anyhow, I suggest that you adopt my example. ASAP, in fact, as things are clearly just about to get worse."

"Um . . . I'm kind of way behind you," I said.

"Hm." He looked at me with a blend of interest and distant pity, like an entomologist considering something in a jar.

"Two things," he said, and he started in, quietly but implacably, like a fortune-teller laying out the pitiless cards.

"That can't be true," I said after he trailed off, gazing sadly out the window behind me. "Is that all true?"

"Have a look," he said. "See for yourself."

So I went to the window, and sure enough, off in the distance were bobbing lanterns, and I could see, as my eyes adjusted, the small line of people straggling down a dirt road toward the water, hauling little carts piled with bundles of stuff.

"They wait all night for the boats, sometimes longer. First come, first serve, I gather. Even a few weeks ago you didn't see this too often, but now there are some almost every night."

Apparently most of the people in the area had lived for centuries by working little farms. But a few years earlier there had been relentless rain, and the flooding had washed out the crops, and then there was a second year of that. The third year was a drought, and so was the next one, so none of the new planting could establish roots, and it all blew away. People were exhausting their stores of food, but then Ray bought up lots of the farms, which, under the circumstances, he got at a very good price. And instead of planting grain or vegetables, he planted eucalyptus, which roots really fast, as a cash crop and to keep the bluffs from collapsing. So everyone was happy for a while. But in the summer there had been a few lightning storms, and the high oil content of the eucalyptus was graphically demonstrated when one of the plantations burst into flame, burning down homes as well as whatever crops were still being grown by anyone who hadn't sold their land to Ray, and food prices were skyrocketing. So naturally local people who could leave were leaving, and a lot of the foreigners, like Ray and Christa, who had places in the area were pulling up stakes, too. "So, that's thing one," Amos said.

"Thing . . . one?" I said.

"And thing two is that Zaffran has rented a place about five miles further up the coast."

"Zaffran? You mean Zaffran the model, Zaffran?"

"Yup."

"But what does that, why should that be, oh."

"Yeah, it started back in the city, it seems. Or that's what Christa seems to think. Zaffran's roshi is near here, and she comes every few months to study with him. She met him when she was here about a year ago, doing that preposterous spread for *Vogue*—all those idylls of her and the donkeys and the beaming peasants with the photoshopped dental work. That's how that whole donkey-ride business started, in fact, with the cute bells and fringe and so on—it was the stylist's idea. And anyhow, that's when she took up Zen. There weren't really any tourists here before the *Vogue* thing, but now there are plenty, so everyone in the village adores Zaffran because the tourist income is about all anybody here has to live on. And a couple of months ago Ray ran into her at some party at home, and she said she needed his advice about buying a place in the area, and, well, so that's the story."

"Oh, God."

"Yeah," he said. "Anyhow, the cook is great, Marya, and she's a real sweetheart. She'll give you food to bring over here and heat up if you don't want to eat at the house."

"Oh, God. Poor Christa. I just can't do that to her."

"Suit yourself," Amos said. "But remember, she'd do it to you."

His point reverberated through my head like a slammed door. I should go upstairs, I thought, and leave him alone to work, but it was hard to move, so just to stall, I asked him what his new show was about.

"Same old, same old," he said. "Never loses its sparkle, unfortunately."

And as Amos began to present the familiar elements and entwine them in a simple moral fable, I began once again to feel that I was falling into a dream. There was the castle, the greedy king, the trophy queen. There were the ravenous alligators, watchfully circling the moat. Soldiers in armor poised at the parapet walls with vats of boiling oil at the ready, and behind them, inside the towers, the king's generals programmed drone aircraft, whose shadows blighted the countryside.

Who was the enemy? Serfs, of course, potentially, who mined underground caves with the help of pit donkeys and brought back huge sacks of gold and jewels to swell the royal coffers. Because what if the serfs and donkeys became inflamed with rage? They were many.

"But what the king and queen don't understand," Amos said, "is that the serfs and donkeys are *already* inflamed with rage, and the bats, who fly between the castle turrets and the mines, are couriers. They're on the side of the serfs, because they love freedom and flying at night and justice, which is blind, too. And the donkeys, once roused, turn out to be indefatigable strategists."

"Huh," I said. "Interesting."

"Yeah? I'm glad. It sure didn't require much thought. But it's got possibilities, I guess."

"What are you going to call it?" I asked.

"What will I call it, what will I call it . . ." His attention seemed to be mainly on one of the little figures, onto which he was gluing something that looked, I noticed, like an orange prison jumpsuit. "Hm. I think I'll call it *The Hand That Feeds You*."

"I'm not sure that's such a—"

"Yes, it is," he said. "It's a great title. Hey, relax, I'll find something more appropriate to call it for this audience."

"So how does it end?" I asked.

"I'm not exactly sure yet, but this is what I'm trying out:

There's a huge popular uprising, and for about three minutes there'll be a rhapsodic ode, during which the serfs, the donkeys, the bats, and the audience rejoice. The end! everyone thinks. But *no,* because there's a second act, and it turns out that the greedy king and queen are only a *puppet* government, keeping a client state in order for an unseen, unnamed greater power."

"You mean, like . . . God?"

"I mean, like, corporate executives. And now that the king and queen have been toppled, a state of emergency has been declared and the laws of the land, such as they were, have been indefinitely suspended, and the corporate executives empower the army to raze the countryside and imprison the bats and the king and queen—everyone, in fact, except the strongest serfs and donkeys, who will continue to toil in the mines, but under worse conditions than before."

"Wow," I said. "That's very . . . that's pretty depressing."

"Well, yeah, sure. But I mean, these are the facts."

"You know, I'm so tired," I said. "Who knows what time it is at home. I think I better go upstairs. Do you have any idea where they keep the water?"

"Here you go," he said, opening a cupboard that held cases and cases of fancy bottled water. "So, good luck with that relaxing thing."

Back up in my room, it seemed to me that I could hear a low, steady rumbling, rising up from the village—just regular night sounds, of course. Just . . . the night sounds of anywhere . . .

I studied the small, white pills Christa had given me. They were not very alarming, swaddled there in their tissue.

They hardly seemed to count. Not that anything else did, either . . .

I woke up not exactly refreshed, more sort of blank, really, as if the night had been not just dreamless but expunged. In fact, where was I? I padded across the unfamiliar floor to the unfamiliar window, and the implausible reality reasserted itself. From here I was looking out at cliffs and the sea, all sluiced in delicate pinks and yellows and greens and blues, as if the sun were imparting to the sleeping rock and water dreams of their youth, dreams of the rock's birth in the earth's molten core, the water's ecstatic purity before it was sullied by life—as if the play of soft colors were the sun's lullaby to the cliffs and the sea, of endurance and transformation.

There was no trace of the people I'd seen the night before from the kitchen window. Could the whole conversation with Amos have been an illusion? There was not a ripple on the glassy water.

A faint jingling was coming my way. I craned out and could just discern one of the local villagers, I presumed, or farmers, wearing loose white clothing and a colorful broad-brimmed hat—leading a procession of little gray donkeys festooned with bells and fringed harnesses and rosettes, picking their way up a steep track, each carrying a big, sack-like tourist.

I wandered over to my laptop, which apparently I'd left on, and called up my e-mail—the Wi-Fi worked, just as Christa had promised—hoping for something to indicate that the world still in fact existed so that someday I might return to it. And—good heavens—there was something from Graham!

All the fragrance from the vines outside blossomed in my room, as though there had just been a quenching rain. Happiness slammed through my body. I, in my desolation—despite the distance, despite our estrangement—had evidently succeeded in calling forth the true Graham, not just the apparition who had come to me in the airport. The lavish air enfolded me, and I breathed it in, expanding as though I'd been constricted in cold shackles for a long, long time. I restrained myself for one more voluptuous second, then opened his e-mail.

> Prisoner? The world is large. You're only a prisoner
> of your own fears. If you don't like it in the prison of
> your fears, go somewhere else. Or stay there if you
> need to. But don't blame me. You obviously expect
> me to be your solution, as if I were an arcane number
> of some sort by which you were neatly divisible. Why
> do you think anybody could be that for you? Why
> do you think anybody could be that for anybody? I'm
> not someone who falls short of me—I'm me. I'm not
> a magic number, I'm just some biped. Look, maybe
> my soul really is dust, but I mean prisoner? Slippers?
> Granary? Of course, I really don't get what you're—

What? "Prisoner"? "Slippers"? "Granary"? Was Graham cracking up over there in Barcelona? And yet . . . Had some fleeting thoughts of mine actually reached him, bent, like little bent darts from Cupid? Or what was happening? I'd begun to tingle, as though I were thinning out, strangely; something strange was happening—Oh! No, no, no, no, no, no, *no*—Graham's note was a response . . . a response to . . . to an e-mail *from me*—apparently sent at *3 A.M.*:

> When you sold me to them, did you envision the consequences for me, the wandering in the tunnels, the sunless life underground, lit only by baskets of cold, glittering gems? What did you hope to gain by divesting me? A subsidiary? Gone are my days of sitting at the hearth, embroidering slippers for the little bats—as innocent as the king and queen are vicious—singing all the whilst I adorned the panels of the granary. Your support for their corrupt regime has cost you more than it has cost me! Yes I am a prisoner now, but your soul has turned to dust, these are the facts. The word "l***," is that what I mean? I "l***" you? I am in a different country and speak a different language, where there is no word for "l***." Oh Graham, Graham, am I going to die here?

And then I finished reading his note:

> —talking about. (As usual, right? I know, I know.) Anyhow, I'm okay, in case you have the slightest interest in the actual me. Barcelona hasn't really worked out, though, so it's time to move on, I guess. Europe is really expensive, and it's hard to get work if you're not a member of the EU. But Africa is mostly in turmoil, and so is Latin America. Australia? What would be the point? China's impossible, and Japan is hurting these days, obviously. Maybe I'll come

back to the States just to regroup for a bit, though god knows it's finished there, isn't it—really, truly finished. Well, I hope you're okay. You really, really don't sound okay. Maybe you should see somebody and get some pills or something. Oh, by the way, I had to sell Blue Hill. I wish I didn't, but I couldn't bring it with me when I moved, and I couldn't afford to put stuff in storage, and I figured that you might get some benefit out of the sale because the buyers were crazy about it and they own a lot of stuff, and maybe the guy will commission you to do a mural for one of his banks, or something. I'll let you know if I'm coming back. Maybe we could get together for a drink. Xo Graham

"Whilst"? I thought—"singing all the *whilst*?" No wonder I couldn't sleep—who would allow themselves to go to sleep, with all the stupid, rotting brain trash that would be waiting for you when you got there! How mortifying, how mortifying—and furthermore, Graham was right; if, in fact, I'd ever l***d him, it was the Graham—his very e-mail made it all too clear—of my own devising. I reread what he had written, and then I read it again, and when I had recovered sufficiently I steamed over to the main house, where I found Christa and Ray at lunch, apparently not looking at each other or speaking. "What the fuck are those pills!" I said. "I wrote someone an e-mail in my sleep!"

Now Ray looked at Christa. "Did you give her one of my Vexnixes? You gave her one of my Vexnixes, didn't you!"

"So what?" she said. "I told you to throw that shit out."

I was just standing there agape. "You gave me some pills that make you *e-mail* in your *sleep*?"

"'*Some*'!" Ray yelled. "You gave her *some*?"

"I'm sorry," Christa said to me, "but you said you were desperate. And they don't do anything to most people."

"They do something to *me*," Ray yelled. "They're the only things that get me to sleep!"

"They fucking decerebrate you!" Christa turned to me. "Ray *drives* in his sleep."

"I do not drive in my sleep!"

"Oh, you're *awake* when you jump in your car at two A.M. and go tearing up the coast to see that loony, anorexic *bitch*?"

"She is *not* anorexic—that's just the way she looks! How many of those things do I have left now?"

"In one second you're not going to have any," Christa yelled, tearing out of the room after him, "because I'm going to flush them down . . ."

And then, happily, both of them were out of sight and earshot. So I helped myself to lunch, and it was all delicious. That night there was the first in a long series of freakish storms, and the sky erupted over and over into webs of lightning that crackled across the water and mountains and valley. Ray didn't show up for dinner, and he didn't show up the next day, either. In fact, he didn't return for nearly a month, during which time Christa alternated between shutting herself up in the bedroom, pounding on my door to talk incoherently for hours, and scaring up whatever expats and aimless travelers she could, for wild parties that lasted days. I was pretty worried about her, especially when I realized she was taking not only Crestilin but Levelal and Hedonalex, too.

When I could, I would hide myself away from the noise and confusion of the parties and ask Marya for meals to bring to the little house for myself. And sometimes Amos and I would stand together at the kitchen window to watch the storms, and the fires springing up on distant slopes. And I would also sneak peeks at Amos, whose face reflected the flames as an entrancing opalescence, as if the light were coming from his lunar skin.

Ray was still gone, and one day Christa came to my room wearing baggy pajamas and carrying a huge armload of beautiful, beautiful dresses. "Here," she said. "These are for you. I don't want them anymore." In her eyes, tears were welling and subsiding and welling. I took the clothes from her, and we stood and looked at each other, and then she turned away and was gone. Naturally, during that time, I thought about Graham quite a bit, and I longed not for him but for the apparition he fell so far short of, which I called up over and over, and gradually wore away until there was nothing left of it, though the loss wasn't exactly a nullity—I could feel an uncomfortable splotch marking its spot, like a darned patch on a sock.

I watched the ravenous flames devouring Ray's eucalyptus, where there had once been small farms and living crops, and I was sorry that I hadn't sent myself my paints and brushes. So Fred drove me to the nearest large town, where I spent most of the frisky money that had made me feel so powerful to acquire some passable materials.

We passed some donkeys on the road, sweet little gray things with eyes as black as Amos's. "Donkeys!" Fred said affectionately.

Fred spoke only a bit of English, so I'm not sure exactly what he was telling me—I think it was that he had a wife and lots of children, and that his wife was a baker, who made the delicious pastries that Marya served every day, but that the price of flour was now so high that the remaining local people could barely afford to buy her bread.

Fred himself was an electrician, I think he said, but these days there wasn't much paying work, so he had started to do any sort of thing he could for Christa and Ray, to make ends meet. I'm not sure, but I think he said that he was helping build a generator, too, for the little hospital in the area, and that there were sometimes electrical emergencies, so he had to drop whatever he was doing for Ray or Christa and go attend to the problem.

Anyhow, he was good at doing a lot of things, and he was kind enough to help me stretch some canvases. Accident had selected me to observe, in whatever way I could, the demonic, vengeful, helpless, ardent fires as they consumed the trees that had replaced the crops—to observe the moment when, at the heart of the conflagration, the trees that sustained it became phantoms, the fire's memory.

In those days I was neither awake nor asleep. The fires, the sea, the parties, Christa, Marya, Amos, and Fred wove through the troubled light, the dusk, the smoky, phosphorescent nights. The water had become rough and gray, and down by the shore a little group of shacks had sprung up, where people waited for a boat to appear on the horizon. Sometimes I thought of my former employer, Howard, just standing there, as I left, not looking at me.

I was getting fed; at home, so was my cat. I arranged to stay another month. Ray returned, and the wild parties came to an abrupt end, though now and again a fancy car would still roar up, and some flashy, drunken teenagers would tumble out at the doors and have to be shooed away. I learned, online, that Zaffran had taken up with a young actor. The first few days Ray was back, he was irritable and silent, but soon he became cheery and expansive, as though he had achieved something of note, and Christa began to make plans to redecorate. "Would you like the dresses back?" I asked. "I don't really have anyplace to wear them." "The dresses?" she said. She smiled vaguely, and patted me, as though I had barked.

Three weeks of drenching rains kept us all indoors, and by the next week, when the rain began to let up, I had completed almost what I could, and Amos was ready to run his show, which he was provisionally calling *State of Emergency*.

The dank fires were still smoldering, and several donkeys had slid into a ravine where they died, heaps of blood and shattered bone, though no tourists had been hurt. With the help of Fred and some kids from the village, Amos had constructed a little theater inside the main house, and we all settled in to watch—Christa and Ray and me, of course, and Marya, and a few Europeans and Saudis, who still had vacation places in the area, and a visitor from Jaipur, who designed software for a big U.S. corporation, and his elegant wife. I wore one of Christa's lovely dresses for the occasion, the only one that didn't make me look seriously delusional.

The curtain rose, over a vibrant and ominous bass line.

You could hear the plashing of the alligators in the moat and the lethal tapping of the computer keys in the towers. A low, queasy buzzing of the synthetic string section slowly amplified as the murky dawn disclosed drone aircraft circling the skies around the castle. Fred had done an amazing job with the lights, and the set, with its beautiful painted backdrops, was so vivid and alluring that sitting there in front of it you felt as though you had been miniaturized and were living in the splendid castle, pacing its red stone floors among the silk hangings. In the caves, where the serfs and donkeys toiled, at a throb of the woodwinds, pinpoints of brilliant yellow eyes flicked open, revealing hundreds of upside-down bats.

Amos had supplied a makeshift recording in his own strange, quavering, slightly nasal voice, of all the vocal tracks laid over an electronic reduction of the score—the forceful recitatives and the complex, intertwining vocal lines. As the conflict built toward a climax, the powerful despots—the king and queen, the generals, and the alligators in the moat—sang of the need for gold and of growing fears. The twilight deepened, and the hills beyond the castle grew pink. Small black blobs massing on them became columns of donkeys and serfs, advancing. The sound of piccolos flared, and Marya grabbed my wrist as a great funnel of dots swirled from the turrets and bats filled the sky, and Amos's quavering voice, in a gorgeous and complicated sextet, both mourned the downfall of the brutal regime and celebrated the astonishing triumph of the innocents.

The curtain dropped, and there was a brief silence until Marya and I began to clap. The others joined in tepidly. "Nicely done, nicely done," the man from Jaipur said.

"We love to have artists working here," Christa said to his elegant wife. "It's an atmosphere that promotes experimentation. Sometimes things succeed and sometimes they fail. That's just how it works."

"That was only the first act," Amos said. "This is intermission."

"Ah," Ray said grimly. "Well, let's all have a stretch and a drink, then, before we sit down again."

"I'm afraid we won't be able to stay for the second act," one of the Saudis said. "An early flight. Thank you. It was a most enjoyable evening, most unexpected."

So the rest of us had a stretch and a drink and sat down for the short second act.

The curtain rose over a blasted landscape. The bodies of the king and the queen swung stiffly from barren trees. With a moaning and creaking of machinery, the ruins of the castle rose unsteadily from the earth. Heaps of smoking corpses clogged the moat.

Three generals, formerly in the service of the hanged royal couple and now in the service of the absent executives, appeared at the front of the stage. One sang of the dangers to prosperity and social health that the conquered rebels had represented. A second joined in, with a lyrical memory of his beloved father, also a general, who had died in the line of duty. And the third sang of a hauntingly beautiful serf rebel, whom he had been obliged to kill.

There was more mechanical moaning and creaking, and up from the earth in front of the castle rose a line of skeletons—serfs, bats, and donkeys—linked by heavy chains. The generals, now in the highest turret, swigged from a bottle of champagne, and as the grand finale, the skeletons, heads bowed, sang a dirge in praise of martial order.

The curtain came down again, heavily. There were another few moments of confused silence, and then Marya and I began to clap loudly, and the others joined in a bit, after which Marya disappeared quietly into the kitchen, to put out the scrumptious dinner she had prepared, and Ray stood up. "Well," he said. "So."

———

I rarely go to parties any longer, but I did go to one the other evening, and there were Ray and Christa, looking wonderful. The milling crowd jostled us together for a moment, and they each gave me a quick kiss on the cheek and moved on, not seeming to remember me, exactly.

In the morning I called Amos, with whom I have coffee now and again, and we arranged to meet up that afternoon. He had just gotten back from touring *The Hand That Feeds You* in Sheffield, Delft, and Leipzig, where it had a modest success, apparently. "Gosh, I'd love to see that show again," I said. "Yeah," he said, "it's changed. I've worked out some of the kinks, and of course I got together some people who can actually sing to record the music, but I can't get it put on here. Too expensive. And my former producer says the stuff about serfs is a cliché."

He was thinner than ever, drawn, actually, and I noticed for the first time that his wonderful, pallid luster had dimmed. "Amos, hey, I really cleaned up with my last show," I said. "Let me take you to a decent dinner."

"Sure," he said, in such a concertedly neutral tone that I realized I'd upset him.

"Wow, Christa and Ray," I said, retreating to more comfortable ground. "I think about them sometimes, don't you? It's odd—no matter how you feel about a place, it's as though you exchange something with it. It keeps a little bit of you, and you keep a little bit of it."

"I know," he said. "And the thing you mostly get to keep is leaving."

A while after we'd both returned home, or so Amos had heard, the last of Ray's eucalyptus trees had been torn out to prevent further fires, and then the bluffs collapsed, sweeping away the remaining huts of the village in mudslides, and Ray and Christa had shut up the place and left, shortly before it was torched. So we wouldn't be seeing it again, obviously, and nobody else would, either.

And in fact it was hard to believe, as we sat there in the rather grubby coffee shop about halfway between our apartments, that the place had ever actually existed, and that Amos had first done his show there that evening when the rains finally stopped and the sky cleared and the stars came out and the moon made a path on the sea that looked as though it led straight to heaven.

No one had mentioned the show at dinner, but there was plenty to talk about that night anyway—a new drug against hair loss that was being developed in Germany, an animated film about space aliens that was grossing an immense profit despite its unprecedented cost, and a best-selling memoir detailing a teenager's abusive upbringing that turned out to have been written by a prankster. And after we'd all had a lot of very good wine and Marya brought out an incredible fruit tart, the man from Jaipur stood to raise his glass and said, "Let us be thankful—let us be thankful for our generous hosts, for art, for this beautiful evening, and for the mild, sunny days ahead!"

Taj Mahal

I was a difficult little boy, and when my mother's chronic illnesses made it impossible for her to care for me, she packed me off to her errant father, the filmmaker Anton Pavlak.

Friends have joked that it was an opportunity for her to punish us both. And when I tell people that I was sent to stay with Pavlak during the heyday of his Hollywood period and I name some of the actresses who were likely to star in the breakfasts I had with him at his home, they look at me as if I'd said that my mother used to send me out to play with lions and tigers.

These episodic visits to my grandfather lasted from the time I was ten until I was nearly fifteen. And it was certainly an eye-opening experience for a child who was used to a sickroom atmosphere and its lonely hush. Even now I find it hard to credit that my joyless, ailing mother *was Anton's child, and that Anton had ever been married to my grandmother, a terrifying old lady with a heavy accent, draped head to toe in black, who appears only in my earliest memories, hovering around my mother's kitchen like a vulture.*

My grandmother had been part of some other life of Anton's, an era and a continent away, back when the two of them and their infant daughter, my mother, were fleeing Europe's gathering storm. The Anton I knew was indeed a brooding, complex figure, but he lived under the bright California sun, in a whirl of colors and flowers and activity.

In Anton's house I was exposed to brawls, tears, romances, scenes, and wild reconciliations. It was a tumultuous time for the tightly knit group of friends who served as the instruments to enact on film my grandfather's dark visions with all their implied violence.

My grandfather could be a tyrant; he was a womanizer. He was often moody and capricious, as his detractors assert. But he was kind to me, though he worked long and intense hours and the daily tasks of seeing that I was fed and clothed fell largely to his household staff.

Whatever my mother's intentions, my times in my grandfather's irregular household were among the brightest of my life. And on nights when I find it difficult to sleep and I sit up watching old movies on TV, the faces of such Olympians as Zoe Sills and Duncan Macgregor appear in the air around me like guardian angels.

I met them there, at my grandfather's: Zoe Sills, Duncan Macgregor, Evangeline Feld, Peter Lofgren,

Coral Durance, Greta Seifert, Roman Karsk, Pansy Resnik, Tara Foley, Luther Kaminsky, and Austin Arles. All of them, and so many others. They were playful and self-indulgent, and, probably because they spent most of their time like children, pretending, they were great fun for a child to be around, even blighted as they were by the famous self-destructive habits and narcissism of actors.

The youngest of them are now old, those who are left. My grandfather passed away decades ago. Evangeline, Pete, Tara, and Zoe are long gone too, and the others are fading away. But I still think of the little gestures of kindness those friends of my grandfather's made to the lonely child I was, and I wish I could repay them now, so many years later.

In fact, this attempt to memorialize my grandfather and his friends, to record these intimate glimpses of their lives, began out of an old debt to Pansy, who found me crying one day when I'd skinned my knee. She took me to her home and cleaned the cut gently and carefully, although I could smell the alcohol on her, and she put a Band-Aid on it. And then we merrily ate too much peppermint ice cream together.

The memory returned to me suddenly not long ago when I attended a Christmas party where peppermint ice cream was served, and I resolved to look Pansy up. After many efforts, I traced her to the dilapidated apartment complex where she was living, neglected, in one room with only a hot plate to cook on. And though she seemed to confuse me with someone else, she clung to my hand and

there were tears in her old eyes, as if some distant memory
was sending its sunny rays into her cloudy mind.

———————

What to do about all this horseshit? Nothing, really, nothing. But still, the ones who are left, those who happen to be in New York—Duncan, Coral, Roman, and Luther—have collected, on this glassily brilliant autumn day, in the noisy bar of a restaurant that Roman likes. Emma has been included, too, although if it weren't for this so-called memoir, these old friends of her mother's would no doubt have forgotten all about her. Even in the book her existence is confined to pages 48, 49, and 316.

"You see, he's *inserted* himself into the story," Luther says, jowls trembling with indignation. "Clement Rouse—who is this putative grandson of Anton's? Whoever he is, it's not his *story*. He's *inserted* himself *into* it."

"Rather a shame his mother *didn't* send him out to play with lions and tigers," Coral says, as the maître d' shows them to their table with a flourish that suggests he's produced it from thin air.

Roman, all wiry eyebrows now, grunts. "Actually it *is* his story, the Clement Rouse story, the story of a guy who thinks he should have gotten to hang out with some people who hung out with his grandfather instead."

"I think *I* should have gotten to hang out with William Shakespeare," Luther says. "Maybe I'll write a book about my intimate glimpses of William *Shakespeare's* life. For heaven's sake—'*Luther Kaminsky and Austin Arles, Luther Kaminsky and Austin Arles*'! All through the damned book it's 'Luther and Austin,' 'Luther and Austin.' What about Luther and *Greta*, please!"

"She was a wonderful woman, Greta," Duncan says. "May she rest in peace." He pats Luther's arm.

They haven't even gotten settled yet, they're still bumping around the table to kiss and embrace Emma, the last arrival. "It's absolutely outrageous," Luther is saying. "It's like something *Greek*—he's assassinating his dead grandfather! This is how people will *remember* Anton's *life*. This is how people will remember *ours*."

Roman grunts again. "Well, in the first place, you can't remember someone else's life."

"I can't remember my own life," Coral says. She takes Emma's face in her hands to survey her with bright, birdy eyes before kissing her on both cheeks. "Hello, Cookie," she says in that familiar whisky voice. "Oh, my. And what is this wild, orgiastic time we were all supposed to be having?" she says to the table in general as she sits down. "What were you guys up to when I was at work?"

These people are near strangers to Emma. They look remarkably dapper, scrubbed clean by age. She hasn't seen any of them for twenty years, since her mother's funeral. And she saw them, and her mother, rarely enough before that. But it's natural that they would have taken the trouble to track down the custodian of Zoe's living genes—she is, after all, another voice to swell their small chorus of lament. Hardy as they clearly are, these old friends of Zoe's are no match for their own clownish simulacra, as reduced and banal as the book's author, arrayed page after page against them: Pansy is *sweet but gaga*, Duncan is *handsome but dull*, Zoe is *lovely but flighty*, Anton is *brilliant but cold*, Roman is *talented but lazy*, Luther is *a pompous ham*, and so on—all of them stamped, sorted, and tossed into bins.

Actually, they happen to be virtuosos of the protean, and their various personae don't adhere even to the normal regulations of chronology. Between reruns, late-night movies, little film festivals, wigs and costumes, any one of them might pop up now at sixty-five, now at twenty-five, now at forty, now an arms dealer, now a doctor, now manning the spaceship, now grooming the racehorse, now striding through corporate headquarters, now stumbling around a saloon . . .

This scene of them around the table, too, could perfectly well be part of a movie, a movie that Emma has been hustled into by mistake. They seem to assume Emma has a role in it, but in fact it's a movie about things that happened to other people long ago.

Ah, thank goodness, coffee. Emma sighs with satisfaction. "Not bad, is it?" Roman says. "I've always found the place reliable."

Though Emma is by decades the youngest at the table, it's her on whom time has set its irrefutable stamp. She has an abrupt sense of how she must look to her mother's friends: *Zoe's child*, impossible! So much taller than Zoe, frown lines and smile lines, a rather severe salt-and-pepper bob—so different from Zoe's yellow dandelion fluff—and absolutely alive at just the age Zoe died.

A shadow swings over her heart, as if she has committed some shameful childish indiscretion, and for a moment she is visiting her mother out west, standing at the sliding glass door and trying not to cry at the sight of the vast, desolate evening, the sun setting instead of rising over the ocean—the wrong ocean—as the purling of the waves washes away the shards of cocktail party noise from inside.

"Emma." A warm hand closes over hers, calling her back through all the years into the restaurant. Duncan is looking at her fondly. He pats her hand: here we are, here we are. Dear Duncan. Her mother's lover.

"All these tourists!" Coral says. And sure enough, all around them people are knocking back various brunch-type cocktails with a tentative, hopeful abandon, as if emulating native ritual.

And the ritual must be working: some minor gods have been made manifest! Smiles ricochet between tables and a few phones are out—There's the dyslexic drug dealer from *Toxins*! And Phil from all those seasons of *Flamingo Park*! And isn't that Coral Whosis, the nurse in those gory movies and the voice of the carrot in *Vegetable Farm*? But, wait, hang on, the colors aren't accurate—these apparitions are . . . *faded* . . . Are they mere projections, imposters, ghosts?

"I can't explain this," Roman says. "Usually it's so civilized. It must have gotten written up somewhere."

"I don't remember Pansy ever drinking much, do you?" Luther says to Duncan. "And her memory is fine. I had dinner with her just last month. There was nothing wrong with her at all."

"Is she really living in one room with a hot plate?" Duncan says. "I must see about that."

"Well, it isn't a palace," Luther says. "But it's perfectly all right, very cozy. And she's *never* cooked. She *hates* to cook."

"But does anyone even remember this grandson of Anton's?" Coral asks. "I mean, *'brawls'*—please! Maybe once someone stamped a foot or two, but *brawls*? Clement Rouse, Clement Rouse . . . can anyone remember any such person?"

"Her eyesight has deteriorated, poor thing," Luther tells Duncan. "That's all."

"Give me her number, will you?" Duncan says. "I'd like to check up on her."

"Would you agree that we were a—what did he say, a 'tightly knit group of friends'?" Coral says to Roman. "Is that what we were?"

"Good question," Roman says. "*Were* we a tightly knit group of friends? Were we a group? Were we friends? Did we even like each other?"

"Well, *you* liked *me*," Coral says brightly, and they crack, wheezily, up.

———

A little boy, all dressed up in a suit, stands in the doorway of Anton's house like a sentinel, staring at Emma. Emma dismounts from her bicycle and stares back. The boy inserts a finger into his nose, as if she can't see him, and then she turns around and rides away.

This can't be quite right, though, Emma's memory. A suit? As if he were making an appearance, at age ten, on a panel of distinguished authors?

There. Now, more convincingly, he's in shorts. His scabby knees are horrible to be seen.

How abominable this book is—cheaply sentimental, stealthily vicious, meretriciously moralizing—a morbidly false soap opera whose coarse innuendoes and simpering calumnies affect to be loving tribute. But what are they supposed to do, ignore it?

Pure gossip and invention! Were any of them interviewed? Were any of them even contacted? No!

"Well, actually, he tried to get in touch with me through my agent," Duncan says. "I'm ashamed to say I ignored the request—I didn't recognize the name."

So, what were the author's sources? The patchy memories, distorted by retrospect and self-flattering fantasies, of a somewhat dull-witted child, bulked up with shoddy interviews, tabloid fabrications, and no doubt any number of biographies and Hollywood memoirs every bit as unreliable as his.

Even for Emma the book is hugely unnerving. Not that Zoe is even remotely the subject, but she does flit conspicuously through the pages, and Emma has been oppressed for days by the feeling of someone's attention, someone's attention trained on her like a sniper's, the feeling that someone has been watching clandestinely, while she's been going about her life . . .

It's not precisely her own life, of course, but in a way this is all the creepier for that. Not someone just watching—someone's grimy hands plunged deep into her foundations, rearranging elements.

"What does it matter really?" Roman is saying. "It's just one more idiotic book by one more idiot."

True, true, the others murmur distractedly, thinking of who knows what—of horrible things that Rouse says about them, of preposterous claims he makes, of shameful things they've actually done that nobody knows about . . .

It has really set things quivering. This morning, crowding into Emma's waking mind were tatters of the late night before—a quantity of alcohol for which she is far too old, an unfortunate encounter, vivid, punishing dreams—and the looming appointment with Zoe's old friends. Almost noon, the clock announced; it had to be kidding. There was a soreness on her skin as if she had been slung into a bag in the rear of a van and driven over rutted roads. She swung her legs out of bed. She could feel the floor's molecular thrum.

It's over and done with, she'd said out loud. Out loud! *It's over and done with.*

But seriously, wasn't that the whole point of the past? The point of the past is that it's immutable.

―――――

"And how is your dear father, Emma?" Coral asks.

"My father?"

"Your father. How is he?"

Her father? How does Coral know her father?

"The last time we were in touch, he had been through a tough bout of pneumonia."

"You're in touch with my father?"

"Oh, not regularly. A card during the holidays, that sort of thing. What a kind man he is."

"Really? No, yes, he is a kind man . . ."

"And good company, too. We used to have so much fun in those years when you were too small to travel by yourself and he would bring you out to see your mother. Of course, he and I disagreed about so many things back then—I always thought he was naïve, you know—an idealist, vulnerable to all kinds of propaganda. But now that the country has dropped utterly into the toilet, I see things quite differently. In any case, it was always very lively, and good fun." She sighs. "It sounds like a dreadful winter. I do hope he's fully recovered."

"Yes," Emma says. Yes, she owes him a visit. She must do that soon.

Zoe Sills had little formal education, but she loved the great novels of former times, even naming her daughter after Jane Austen's spunky heroine, Emma. Zoe was often to be found posed on a divan, all wrapped up in a soft throw, reading. But Anton, an intellectual and a good thirty years her senior, never took her seriously.

The truth is that there was never anything more between them than the inevitable generic attraction between power or talent (in Anton's case, both) and beauty. Anton cared more about his films than about any mere humans, and perhaps he was too arrogant to realize what would surely happen when he cast Zoe opposite Duncan Macgregor in Chameleon, *or too egocentric. But if he couldn't see what was happening in front of him in real life, he came face-to-face with it during one fateful*

evening's screening of the day's rushes, as the dailies were
called back then.

They were all sitting in the screening room: Anton,
the script girl (as the continuity person was called back
then), Zoe, Duncan, Ruffle Anselm, who designed the
costumes, and of course Kurt Schoenfeld, Anton's famous
cinematographer. And there was that unconcealable nervous excitement in the air that there always is when movie
people are about to find out what it was the camera saw
them do that day.

The first two scenes they watched were simple—Zoe
alone, walking along under the leaves at twilight. It was
just snippets of raw footage, but rough as it was, the scenes
were clearly successful, starkly ominous. You could see every
thought, every sensation playing over Zoe's perfect face.

While the clips unspooled in front of them, Zoe's hand
was on the arm of Anton's chair, as if she wanted to touch
him, to make some kind of contact with him, as if she
wanted his reassurance. But Anton's hands were occupied
with a pen and a pad of paper so he could make notes, and
every fiber of his being was focused on the small screen.
Duncan Macgregor was sitting just a little off to the side,
in front of Zoe.

The third scene, the big scene of the day, was longer
and more complex. Many takes were shot. It was the famous scene in which Zoe's character catches a glimpse of
the stranger, played by Macgregor, for the first time. He
is partially hidden by trees, doing something, and after a
while we see, as Zoe does, that he's digging. His shirt is
lying crumpled near his feet; an agitated dog is nipping

at him. If Zoe keeps walking, she will come into his line of vision. She stops stock-still to watch. The intensity he projects is terrifying but riveting.

Some little thing goes awry in each of the first many takes. Zoe stumbles then giggles, the spade slips and Macgregor swears, the dog gets distracted and goes wandering off, Zoe visibly stifles a sneeze, a helicopter wobbles into the shot, and so on. "Take eight!" "Take nine!" "Take ten!"

On film the actors are becoming tense and stiff. In the screening room everyone is on edge. Even if they could budget in an extra day to shoot the scene again, the dog has another commitment. Zoe sighs loudly, as if to express and thus diffuse the general anxiety, but none of the other viewers respond.

It was take thirteen, the final take, that told the whole story. In the few seconds of film that remained after Anton had yelled "Cut," everyone assembled in the screening room witnessed the two gorgeous and magnetic actors let loose and laugh, knowing they've finally gotten a whole flawless take. And then, as the last few frames flicker out, their gazes meet, fuse, and ignite.

There was total silence in the screening room. Neither Zoe nor Macgregor moved a muscle. It must have been nearly thirty full seconds before Anton spoke. "Let's see that one again, please," he said. His tone was level, and chilling. "Let me see take thirteen again."

"I certainly don't remember that," Duncan says. "Wasn't it after *Chameleon* was finished that your mother and I got together?" He looks at Emma, as if for confirmation, but how on earth would she know?

And how would Clement Rouse know? It's safe to say that Clement, who would have been five or six when *Chameleon* was made, was not in the screening room that evening. Or, probably, ever.

Duncan frowns. "Yes, I'm sure it was later. I don't think Zoe and I gave each other much of a thought until *Splice*. And she and Anton were living apart by then, anyhow."

———

How would anybody know anything about anybody?

Emma sighs and brushes a dark hair off her sleeve, as if she were brushing away a loose filament of the tattered web spun out since Adam and Eve between the little figures continually replenishing across the earth's surface.

"Isn't it wonderful?" Luther says, as the waiter hurries from one of them to the next, setting down immense breakfasts. "We've lived long enough for eggs to be healthy again."

"All those years when they were considered pure poison," Duncan says.

"Oh, yes," Coral says. "You were supposed to flatten yourself against the wall if you saw one approaching."

"What about hollandaise, I wonder," Luther says. "Is that healthy now, too? And bacon?"

"Oh, I think we're too old for bacon to kill us," Roman says.

———

"The Mouse is coming over to play, be nice to him, sweetheart, won't you? I think he has a great big crush on you."

That's right: Zoe recruited Clement the Mouse to come over and play with Emma. Or, as he seemed to interpret his function, to boss her around. The Mouse scrabbled and flinched, but he must have been—must be—two or three years older than she, a significant difference back then. That poor Mouse—bully as he clearly is by nature, it was probably the only opportunity he'd had thus far to boss anyone around.

That hair of his! Hair of no color whatsoever, like some sort of cellulose packaging. And his gruesomely bitten fingernails, and his sad little face, like a knot of grubby string . . . Oh! And that dress of her mother's, splashed with delicious pink flowers . . .

Milk and cookies—the white cloth spread out on the dainty tea table, the milk and the porcelain plate glimmering white, almost equally liquid in all that sunshine, the dirty mouse paws with their scratches and Band-Aids, the hypnotic glitter of the ocean, a vase of peonies, the cookies, the lawn . . .

Two strays, propped up opposite each other at a tea table, wondering what on earth they're supposed to do. There's the milk, there are the cookies. This moment, always this moment, the eternal threshold—all the preparation: learning to walk, learning to talk, how to tell time, how to tie your shoes, learning about stars and continents and dinosaurs, and now she and the Mouse are sitting across from each other.

So, you're born, and then what? Outside, the ocean glitters. From here on, it's all wide and empty, you can't see where the water meets the sky, you can't see what's written on the pale sheet of air. The sun's magnificent salvos announce each day and its close—one by one the unprecedented, irretrievable sheets of writing are revealed, then discarded. The Mouse stares fixedly at the cookies, then grabs one.

By the time I arrived in California, Zoe and Anton were on good terms again, and although she had left Anton for Duncan Macgregor a few years earlier, I often saw her around Anton's house. She had sent for her little girl, Emma, who lived in New York with her mentally unstable father, and at last mother and daughter were reunited in something like a real family, with Macgregor. Emma was a shy child, stiff and awkward, nothing like the ebullient, lighthearted Zoe.

No one who ever saw the radiant Zoe Sills in person could forget her. She was even more beautiful in person than she was on-screen. And truly, she was so ethereal that at the age of ten, I seriously half believed she was a fairy.

From the first glimpse I caught of her, I imagined doing something bold, like gathering roses from my grandfather's garden to make a bouquet for her, as if I were a medieval knight in armor. So imagine my astonishment when she approached me—a ten-year-old boy!—and invited me to the tastefully luxurious home overlooking the ocean that she shared at that time with Macgregor.

Her mentally unstable father! Where on earth did Clement get that one? Apparently from the same overstocked storehouse of substandard goods, his imagination, where medieval knights staggered around, clanking, in hundreds of pounds of armor, plucking roses!

Besides, Anton *loathed* roses. In fact, as Emma remembers, he made quite a to-do about growing only wildflowers. If a rose had ever managed to breach the ramparts, the gardener would have had to fall on his fucking halberd!

At home in New York, something was wrong. The rent had gone way up, her father said. The two of them moved in with Sandi, and Emma was to share a room with the two little kids until her father found a new apartment. Sandi was kind, but on the TV soldiers were trapped in a jungle with explosions and people were dying and dying, not like a movie, there was no ending, and her father couldn't stop watching. What were they doing? He just shook his head.

She was old enough to go on the plane by herself for the first time. Yes, now she remembers—on the plane alone. Her father had let her pick out a little suitcase. The consolingly familiar surfaces of the plane, its seats and the armrests that could move, arriving into the lush air, the sunsets shimmering in the fringes of the palm trees, Zoe's pink dress, empty days, milk and cookies . . .

There was a bicycle. Sometimes she rode over to Anton's house, where she had stayed on visits when she was little, but her old friend was working on a movie. The housekeeper, Flora, would visit with Emma, and let her roam around the sunstruck rooms that were so familiar and yet so unfamiliar. Hello, house. Did it remember her?

And then there was the day when the boy with the colorless hair and scabby knees was standing in Anton's doorway and Emma stopped at the bottom of the driveway and they stared at each other and she turned around and bicycled back to Zoe's.

And there was the day, it must have been earlier, when Zoe took her shopping. They were all going to go out to dinner, Emma, Zoe, and Duncan, and why hadn't Emma brought a party dress with her, Zoe said. "Close your mouth, darling, a fly will get in. You'll need something pretty tonight. What was that crazy father of yours thinking?"

They went to a shop and the lady there hugged Zoe, and Zoe picked out some dresses. There was a white cotton one. "Just look at that precious eyelet!" the lady said, and when Emma tried it on, the lady almost cried, she said, because Emma looked like a princess. Emma looked at Zoe.

Zoe considered, and nodded. "All right," she said. "We have to do something about your hair, darling, but that'll have to wait until I can get you to Philippe." Eyelet? "This," Zoe said, indicating the magical little holes that made the dress look like it was floating.

Later, it must have been later, that afternoon, Emma went out to ride her bike, but when she came back to the house, Zoe was slamming around. "Serena Lassiter! Can you believe it? Serena Lassiter—that vile girl! And this is the second part, the second one! That's not acting, that's *mime*. You can see that girl coming around the corner."

Duncan was darkly silent as Zoe stuffed Emma roughly into the delicate new dress. "Serena Lassiter does not look one week younger than I do!" Zoe was in no mood to go out, she had changed her mind—settled. Did she want to see any of those people? But Emma and Duncan were to go, nonetheless. She herself needed some privacy, please—some quiet.

It was hard to sit in the car without creasing her new dress. Duncan said not to worry. At the restaurant they got out of the car and a man in a uniform got into it. Duncan came around to her side to help her out. Inside there were carpets and candles, and the soft chime of glass, laughter, silver, china. Behind the tall windows the palms swayed, and tossed their graceful branches.

Back at the house, Zoe might be crying, but maybe it was best not to remind Duncan. He was cheerful, and handsomest of everyone there. He let her have a sip of his cocktail. The waiters brought her special things and spoke to her tenderly, as though she were soon to ascend the throne.

If only she had a picture to show her father! Was there a postcard, she wondered, but she couldn't explain to Duncan. You could never tell about her father, anyhow. Sometimes he didn't like very nice things. Polluted, he said.

"Do you remember that photo of Zoe in my father's play?" Emma asks Coral.

"What? No—what play? That's right, I'd forgotten he wrote plays."

"Oh, he used to," Emma says. "He gave up."

"I remember that picture," Duncan says. "It was up on her wall for a while, yes?"

"I wonder what ever happened to that," Emma says.

"She looked so young . . . ," Duncan says.

"Well, it would have been the early 1960s," Emma says. "They were in college. Zoe was only a sophomore." Her father stands triumphantly on a stage in front of a crowd; his dark hair is still neatly cut and he wears a white shirt with a button-down collar, but his fist is raised, and the young faces looking up at him are rapt. Standing next to him, dewy, flushed, haloed with joy, and invisibly pregnant, is Zoe. "I'm in that picture, too, actually," Emma says.

The occasion is the curtain call at the first performance of the play Emma's father wrote called *Emma in the New World,* an imagining of Emma Goldman's reflections while she was on trial for inciting to riot.

"Zoe as Emma *Goldman?*" Coral says.

"She would have been very good as Emma Goldman," Luther objects.

"Indeed," Roman says.

"Oh, she could do anything, your mother," Luther says. "She could be anyone. And she could make even the most vacuous, inconsistent, clichéd nonsense seem plausible."

Yes, there was her mother curled up on a sofa, no makeup on, as if she could absorb a part better without it, studying a script hour after hour.

"She always seemed to believe that there was a real person locked away in the words, no matter how inane," Duncan says. "It was always as if she was rescuing somebody lost there, or imprisoned."

"She never really got the credit she deserved," Luther says. "The only thing people ever talked about was how pretty she was."

"Oh, I know," Coral says. "Zoe was simply amazing. But

Emma Goldman! For one thing, she was far too pretty." And Emma has to laugh a bit, too.

Duncan Macgregor owes his reputation as an actor to his appearance. If you analyze his performances you will see that they consist largely of standing still. He has portrayed on film nine senators, seven of them fictitious, and three congressmen. Add to that his stage appearances as two more members of Congress. Out of all these, only one was corrupt, an unlikely average.

After Anton returned to Europe in the mid-1980s, Macgregor's lucrative but unadventurous career thrived. Others who had habitually worked with Anton fared less well. A number of those who had appeared in his early movies, such as Peter Lofgren and Tara Foley, had already passed away. And a new breed of directors, much younger men, notably Kenneth Pell and Rick Heaton, now dominated the public imagination. These directors had been profoundly influenced by Anton, they had learned from him, they had copied his tricks, they revered him, and audiences had forsaken him for them.

Still, no other director seemed to be able to use his performers as effectively. And in his roles during that period, Kaminsky in particular, a very broad actor, is unconvincing, even ludicrously miscast. Zoe Sills had long outgrown her niche as ingenue, Pansy Resnik took on a series of trivial parts in B movies, and Coral Durance (who was rumored to have been an old rival of

Zoe's from their days of closeness to Anton) defected to New York, to work in theater, for which she had originally trained. Roman Karsk, whose performances never rose above workmanlike solidity, faded away entirely.

"Coral, do you mind if I ask you something?" Emma says.

"You are asking me something, Emma dear."

"Did you ever actually have a fling with Anton?"

"I might mind answering, though."

"You *did* have an affair with Anton?" Roman says.

"Of course not," Coral says.

"You wouldn't lie to me, of course," Roman says.

"Of course not," Coral says again. "But I might lie to Emma."

"I can't believe this!" Roman says.

"I'm just joking," Coral says.

"*You* two?" Emma, wide-eyed, asks Coral and Roman.

"Of course not," they say in unison.

Well, who is Emma to judge?

They all concur: much of the stuff in the book about Anton's early life probably is true, or at least is something that Rouse might have been told, by his mother if not by Anton; Zoe had alluded more than once, when Emma was young, to the hair's breadth escapes, the wandering and hiding in the forests during the carnage, starving and stealing, laboring for the farmer under cover of night in the frozen field, the bribes, footsteps approaching the closet door, the forged passport . . .

And it is surely the case that back there, way back before all the other women, there was Clement's grandmother, fleeing, on the boat over with Anton, and that Anton made his way to California's sunlight without her, by sheer will and brains and nerve, and started right off with cameras.

Anton. The nice scratchy feel of his jacket when he picked her up, his laugh! How could that Anton have disappeared from Emma's mind this whole time? Immensely old, courtly, remote, cryptic, ironic, fastidious . . . that accent of his! When she was little she craved hearing it, as if it was a special language that conveyed only the most important things.

Well, no mystery about why he'd left Europe. And if the accounts are to be credited, he was the only one from his family who managed to. The mystery is why he returned.

"After half a century," Duncan marvels.

"Well, for instance, my dear late wife injured her knee in a childhood accident," Roman says. "And the whole rest of her life she could tell what weather was coming,"

"He knew perfectly well how fast things can happen," Coral says. "People always say, 'Oh, things might not be great here, but it's stable, our problems are ordinary.' You know. And the next thing you know, laws are gutted, the economy comes crashing down, people are in the streets, it's all the fault of the ones with beards or the ones without beards, or whoever . . ."

"And he was sick of the pressure to make huge profits," Roman says. "The big budget money. He was sick of the marketing and sick of having to meet with idiots and trying to explain what he was doing. Really sick of it." Absently, he picks up the salt shaker, weighing it in his hand.

"Well," Duncan says. "Anyhow, those are the sorts of things people tell themselves. Explanations. You know."

"I suppose people always want to go home," Emma says.

"Even if they've never had a home in the first place," Coral says.

"And there would have been that other thing," Roman says.

"What other thing?" Duncan asks.

"That other thing. You know, the now-or-never thing."

Grainy rather than glossy, sepia lighting, the movies Anton ended up making in Europe, though more overtly harsh, weren't too different from the ones he had made in America. There were the misleading clues, the tightening spirals of danger, approaching footsteps, neighbors inexplicably appearing, reflections in mirrors or puddles or windows, obstructed views . . .

The European movies were as misinterpreted as the American ones had been, and briefly they were as popular. Then audiences in both Europe and America moved on to simpler, noisier, and less troubling movies.

"They look very good now," Duncan says. "I happened to see a couple of them recently. In my opinion, they're due for a serious reevaluation."

"What were you up to in those years?" Luther asks Roman. "I lost track of you for quite a while there."

"Oh, me," Roman says. "Well, I suddenly couldn't stand *any* of it." "The auditioning, the stupid parts, waiting for the phone to ring—with all due respect, what kind of life is that for a grown man? So I decided to grow tomatoes instead."

Coral smiles. "Remind me. How did that work out for you?"

Roman spreads his hands in a shrug. "Who wants a life for a grown man?"

Amazing—eighty-some years old, and they're sort of flirting, Emma thinks. Good news. Or maybe not.

"Heavens," Luther says. "Can you believe that all that turned out to be *then*? At the time I somehow thought that it was *now*. Did it occur to you that it was going to be *then*?"

"It didn't need to occur to me," Roman says. "I already knew it."

"But Luther means, did it *occur* to you," Coral says.

"Well, no," Roman says. "Of course it didn't occur to me."

"Aren't you going to finish that bacon?" Luther asks Duncan.

"Please," Duncan says. "Help yourself."

"Why don't you and Duncan get married one of these years?" Emma remembers asking once. She was visiting. It was a few years after Anton had pulled up stakes, and she and Zoe were sitting in a café that served big salads Zoe liked.

"I don't want to get married again, darling," Zoe said. "Why should I get married? I was married to your father. That was quite enough of that. I want my independence, I like having my own little house. Duncan and I are very happy as we are. And this way, if he goes off one day with some young girl, I won't have the humiliation of being the wretched old wife."

No, but they weren't in that café, Emma thinks—they were

in Zoe's house, because there was a little stack of scripts at the side of a sofa. "You don't know what it's like, darling, getting old. Look at those—all trash. Foolish busybodies, despicable mothers-in-law, horrible gargoyles, pathetic trolls, there are two bedridden souses somewhere in there . . . Every once in a while something comes in with a *noble* old hag, some plucky old *hag*, and how *moving*, how *inspiring* it is that despite her advanced years she's finding solace and purpose in, what, in, I don't know, in raising warthogs."

"Forty-two is not old," Emma said.

"Thirty-six, darling. Maybe in that East Coast paradise of yours a woman of my age is not all that old, but here I might as well be a thousand. A thousand! Thirty-six? It's big news out here that women live that long! Just yesterday I got a call about something in which I'd be Austin Arles's mother, can you imagine? Austin is five years older than I am! I mean of course I'll *take* it. They'll add a few wrinkles, I'll dodder."

Emma sighed.

"Not that it's a *large* degrading part, naturally it's a degradingly *small* degrading part. Oh! You can seriously not know what it's like to become old."

"If I'm lucky I'll get to find out one of these days," Emma said.

"But, no, darling, seriously. Of course it's not so important if men don't find you attractive any longer. That's not an important thing. What's important is—what's important, what's very, very important, is to make a place for yourself on the planet, your own little place. To do your work. You think people can't take that away from you, but they can."

"Men still find you attractive, Zoe."

"Why don't you call me Mother, darling? You never called me Mother even when you were a little girl. You were so sweet, darling, but you never called me Mother. I know what you think, you think, my mother is a silly woman, a superficial woman. My mother is just depressed because she's lost her looks and men don't find her attractive any longer, but Emma darling, do you think that took me by surprise? I'm not an imbecile. I was the pretty girl, but as long as I worked with Anton, I could do things that had some substance. Now, all that's available is the old hag with no substance whatsoever. And even if you're good enough to *be* the old hag, even if you have the stamina to wait it out, there are years of purgatory before you're allowed even that.

"But the worst thing is that you're just not exactly part of the world any longer. When you're young, everyone is holding hands, all your friends, even the people you don't like, everyone in the world, but at a certain point, when you get older, you float a little off the surface of the earth. Everyone is rising up off the surface of the earth, everyone is farther away from one another—you can't hold hands any longer, you stretch out your hand, but you can't reach anyone else's, and when you look down, you see that what you thought was the world is just a wrapping around the world, a loose, disintegrating wrapper, with a faded picture of the world on it. The world is where young people live."

"You haven't lost your looks," Emma had said. "Don't be ridiculous."

"Oh, I know you won't be silly like me when you come to be my age."

"What if you'd had to spend your life working on an assembly line in a meat-packing plant?" Emma said. "What if you lived in a mining town where the air is poison and the men die underground tearing minerals and fuel out of rock—Mother? What if you always had to get up while it was still dark to gather firewood and fetch water from the stream miles away? What if the plantation was taking your little subsistence farm, what if the bank was taking your little house? What if there were always managers watching to see if you fulfilled your quota of stocking shelves or slinging burgers or checking out T-shirts? What if you'd been sold? What if you picked fruit in the scalding sun fourteen hours a day and lived in a trailer with six other people who were citizens nowhere? What if planes flew overhead all day every day, dropping bombs on your village? What if you lived any of the lives lived by most of the people in the world?"

"Well, I don't, darling, do I. Like everybody else, I live the life that *I* live. We're each allotted the life of one particular person. We don't choose it. I've had very good luck, I know that. And, frankly, darling, so have you. As it happens, you don't work in a meat-packing plant, either. As I remember, you've just gotten yourself a lovely job with the Parks Department." Zoe's gaze was brief, irritable, final, as if Emma were only an annoying memory she was dispensing with.

Emma remembers that look. She remembers it. Over and over, it makes something inside her tear, like the lining of an old, useless coat.

"Ah, well," Zoe had said, "you come by it honestly."

"What?" Emma demanded. "I come by what honestly?"

"I never should have let you live with that gloomy, censorious, sanctimonious father of yours—never."

"Darling!" Zoe said when Emma announced she was getting married. "How exciting, how wonderful! I'm so happy for you. How soon do I get to come to New York and meet your gent?"

Emma pictured Zoe at the other end of the phone, blinking back the tears that she produced so easily when a script required her to. "Hey," she said, "since you think marriage is so great, don't forget that Duncan is still on those lists every year of the world's most desirable bachelors."

"Oh, please. But darling, I'll make you and Ed a big, beautiful wedding."

"No," Emma said. "I want to get married at City Hall."

"I want to get married at City Hall," Emma told Ed later.

"But, Emma," he said. "Would you really deny your mother this pleasure?"

"I don't want a *wedding*, I want a *marriage*. She's just playing with dolls."

Looking back, seeing the aggrieved expression on Ed's face, another face that looks so young from this distance, it seems obvious that Ed had basically believed himself to be marrying Zoe, not her.

But Zoe came to New York anyhow, to help them, as she put it, celebrate, bringing various extravagant, ornamental, useless little gifts, which Emma eventually left behind in Ed's apartment, along with Ed.

The night before they went to City Hall, when Emma arrived after work at the lavish restaurant where Zoe was treating, Zoe and Ed were already deep into a bottle of some splendid wine, and Zoe was sniffling beautifully. She dried her eyes, also beautifully, and kissed Emma. "Oh, don't mind me," she told Ed, and Ed actually touched his pocket hanky to her face.

"What was that all about?" Emma asked when she and Ed got back to their apartment.

He looked at her coolly, speculatively, as if she were his teenage child being released by the police into his custody. "She's a very sensitive person. She's very fragile. It's understandable that she'd be very emotional on this occasion."

"She's an actress. She was *embodying* sensitivity. She was *embodying* fragility."

"Really, Emma, I can't imagine what makes you think you're always right."

"Since when do you have a pocket hanky?"

"Naturally, I wanted to dress appropriately for your mother," Ed said.

And the next day, when dear Sandi, who never flashed around embodiments of anything, had a party for them at her tiny place, Ed behaved as if he were graciously allowing the peasants to bring them garlands in the pigsty.

Ed and his *career*! A career for him, a *job* for her. Did she not work like a dray horse and come home to cook and to clean? Well, how could he cook or clean—he had a *career*, as opposed to her *job*, to attend to.

And eight years later, when she confessed to Zoe that there was serious trouble between herself and Ed and that she was seeing someone she'd met, a liaison between the mayor's office and the Parks Department—a dynamic, adventurous, astute, and charming man—Zoe raised an eyebrow. "Really," she said. "I see."

Emma had not used the words *handsome* and *married*, but Zoe had known just what she'd meant. "Well, I'm sorry, but you're bound to wake up soon, darling, wondering what happened to you."

Naturally Zoe was right. How could Emma have been such a stooge? "Dynamic, adventurous, astute, and charming." She winces; she'd actually used those exact words, she thinks. And it wasn't for a long time—some time, in fact, after Avery had moved on to another woman—that the sparkling haze finally blew off the thought of him.

By then, of course, Emma's marriage was nothing but rubble. Well, that marriage was prefab rubble! What but rubble could it ever have become? "Darling, what are you doing at home on a Saturday night?" Zoe apparently called to ask. "You're an attractive young woman—you should be going out and having fun!"

And when Emma runs into Avery, as she does, inevitably, from time to time at events like last night's—events at which she more or less has to show her face, where practical alliances are formed, damaged, or reinforced, events that are more tournament than dinner party (who has survived, who has been disgraced, whose status excites envy, whose pity? Who has a new condo, who has a new wife?)—she feels nothing more than a dull rage: when something is unfair, it's unfair again, because there's just nothing at all you can do to make it fair.

How easily Avery had introduced her, just last night, to a very young, very beautiful woman, lacquered to a high, impermeable gloss—his new wife.

———

Well, it's over and done with, she said out loud this morning. As if anything were ever over and done with! Oh, but could she not even spend the morning in bed, snoozing a bit? No, she could not; she had to get up to meet Zoe's friends. And now here she is with them because Clement Rouse has altered some bit of the past—he unlocked some door and out popped this highly improbable day.

———

There came a point when Zoe stopped calling. A relief for a time, then a concern. Emma conferred with Duncan; he was mostly at his place in Idaho in those days, but still in daily touch with Zoe. He was concerned, himself; Zoe seemed anxious and distracted.

Emma flew out to see her. "Are you eating anything, Zoe?" she said. "You're too thin. Are you all right?"

"I'm fine, darling. I just don't seem to have much energy. And it makes me sad that there are so many things I've missed out on in my life."

"What are you talking about? You have a very full life."

"I did at one time, I suppose. What do I have now?"

"Well, I mean . . . you still get parts, you—"

"A few parts," Zoe agreed. "A very few. All contemptible."

"You have . . . well, you have me . . ."

Zoe had looked at her blankly.

"Me?" Emma said. "Remember? Your child?"

"Ah, my—I wish I'd had a lot of children."

"Me too."

"Well, darling, it's not too late. If you'd only find a nice man to marry."

"No, I meant—"

"One who isn't married already. You were so adorable. I really should have had more *children*. There are *so* many things I've missed. I wasted so much time! I've never read *War and Peace,* can you believe that?"

"I'll get you a copy of *War and Peace* tomorrow, Zoe."

"I've read so little. I always had so many scripts to read—I never had time. I wish I'd read *War and Peace,* I wish I'd read *Oliver Twist* and *Moby-Dick* and *Pride and Prejudice,* all those wonderful books."

"Have you seen a doctor, Zoe?"

"Why should I see a doctor—there's nothing wrong with me. I just regret not having done more in my life. Emma, I've hardly traveled at all."

"It's not possible to do everything. No one can do everything. You've worked very hard, Zoe. It's not possible to work and to have a wonderful life at home and to go off traveling at the same time."

"I ought to have traveled, at least. Isn't it a waste to die before you've seen the Alhambra? Or the Taj Mahal?"

"A waste of what? Zoe, are you taking some kind of pills? If you're taking some kind of pills, they're not doing what they ought to be doing!"

"How long do you plan on staying, darling?"

"Why not pack a suitcase right now and get on the phone

and get yourself a ticket to India. You could see the Taj Mahal this *week*. I'll go with you. We can go visit the Taj Mahal together."

"Very sweet of you to offer, darling. I'm sorry that one day I'll die without ever having seen the Taj Mahal, but I really just don't have it in me at the moment."

"What *are* you talking about, Zoe? Stop taking whatever it is you're taking, and go to the Taj Mahal! Meantime, why don't you call someone, one of your friends?" Emma pleaded. "Why don't you call Duncan? He wants to see you."

"He doesn't want to see me," Zoe said.

"He wants to see you. So does Coral, I spoke to her. So does Luther. So does Greta. So does Austin. So does Roman. Everyone wants to see you."

"They don't want to see me."

"They do. They all want to see you."

"I don't want to see them."

"Zoe, please. Mother."

"I want to see Anton."

"Anton is dead, Mother. I'm sorry. Don't you remember?" Emma's heart had started to pound. "Anton went to Europe, and he died there a few years ago."

"I know. I want to see Anton."

Zoe closed her eyes and lay back on the sofa. Emma moved over to sit beside her and took her hand. "Should I get us some tickets to India?"

Zoe laughed. "Darling, what for? Just let me lie here and yearn to see the Taj Mahal. Really, Emma, when you die, you don't know whether you've seen the Taj Mahal or not."

That particular generation of successful American actors was lucky. They lived richly, in the sunshine, and they made some notable movies. Now the industry has been all but destroyed by digital techniques and global economic trends. The creative energy is now in low-budget independent films, or television, which has largely moved East. The sunny bower those people lived in is gone.

But there still is television and independent film, and for those who are trained for it, the stage. So some of those from Anton's set have given up the comforts of Southern California for the harsh climate of New York, to spend their old age doing the only thing they've ever known.

Coral Durance, despite two hip replacements and a dependence on painkillers, made a great success on the Broadway stage as the wise grandmother in Harvest Day. *Roman Karsk can still be seen doing his Mafia don in season after season of* Tarantella. *Luther Kaminsky's comeback in the surprise hit* Potluck, *which showed his broad style to advantage, maintains an apartment in New York as well as his old place in the Hollywood Hills, and is spotted at fashionable events. After Zoe died, Duncan Macgregor returned from his self-exile in Idaho, and now leads the quiet life of a squire in his home overlooking the Pacific Ocean, where presumably, before too long, he'll end his days.*

When that great talent Anton Pavlak died, he left to me a beautiful Viennese desk, which I like to imagine had once belonged to his family, long before the dark days in Europe. He knew that I had admired that desk even when I was a child, and perhaps he pictured me as I would be so many years later, sitting at it to memorialize my times with him.

After a rapid and fierce battle with cancer, Zoe Sills succumbed. I made great efforts to visit her toward the end, but I failed. She had shut herself away, I was told by her attendant, a very handsome and slippery young man, and she was seeing no one at all. It is very likely that he was more or less keeping her a prisoner, driving a wedge between her and those who loved her, in hopes of inheriting her money. He did, however, on my final attempt, bring out a note to me signed shakily in her hand: "For dear Clement, I wish you nothing but happiness in your life." I will treasure that relic until my own dying day.

More coffee for anyone? No? "Thanks, we'll just settle up," Roman tells the waiter.

Be not afraid. Be of good cheer. Though you walk through the valley of the shadow of—"Do you think Zoe knew she was sick before she was really debilitated?" Emma asks.

Duncan nods. "I believe she had a strong intuition."

"Oh, yes," Coral says. "Otherwise she never would have burned her letters when she did."

"Her letters?" Emma says.

"Her letters?" Duncan says.

Coral looks at him. "Well?" she says.

"Very strange," Emma says. "I didn't know there were letters. And Rouse doesn't say anything about them."

"How would he have known about them?" Coral says. "Even if he had ransacked the little bungalow where she was living at the end, he wouldn't have found any. We burned them."

"'We'?" Emma says.

Coral shrugs. "Trevor helped."

"A good kid, Trevor," Duncan says. "Huh, letters . . ."

"Do you know, she actually did manage to leave him a little," Emma says. "It was very sweet. She was so broke there at the end, but she split up the tiny bit left between me and Trevor, as if we were brother and sister."

"He certainly took good care of her," Luther says. "So many people clamoring to get in to see her."

"Oh, yes, he was great," Roman says. "He wouldn't let a soul in who she didn't want to see."

A silence has fallen over the table. Emma looks at her mother's friends. Their old age seems provisional, a temporary blurring or slackening of outlines. Here in the dim restaurant they appear to be indistinct embryonic forms, waiting with patience and humility to be issued new roles, new shapes. They all seem to be thinking, considering, dreaming a little, floating halfway between heaven and earth. Coral's hand extends slightly and opens, as if to take someone else's—

"Excuse me! Excuse me!" someone is shouting, and something that's bumping at Emma's shoulder turns out to be a large rear end that belongs to someone from another table who is looming over them with his phone out. "Excuse me," the person, rear end to Emma's shoulder, is shouting apparently at Luther, "I hate to interrupt, I wanted to wait till you were finished, but do I know who you are?"

"Well," Luther says, as his face arranges an amiable but regretful smile, "eh—"

"I know that voice—it's you, isn't it!" The man shouts, as if Luther were in another realm. "Wait, don't tell me—am I wrong? No, I know you, don't I? I know you! All right, I give up, what's your name?"

"Em, Luther Ka—"

"Right, that's right, you used to be Luther Kaminsky! Listen! My kids were huge fans of *Potluck* when they were little, they'd never forgive me if I didn't get a picture. God, that was so damn funny, where you were running all the way up in the Empire State Building in your underwear!"

"Eh—" Luther chuckles vaguely and ducks his head apologetically to his distinguished colleagues as he rises stiffly from his chair. "Maybe, em, maybe over there where we're not in everybody's . . ."

Watching Luther and his admirer getting photographed together by the waiter, Roman and Coral smile a little. Luther has been vocal about *Potluck,* about how humiliated he felt to sink to its level, but this stranger is beaming with joy. Who could help feeling good about that?

"Well." Luther returns to the table, looking a bit sheepish, and they all stand up, shake themselves out, and head to the coat check.

"By the way, I'll be doing Lear next fall," Luther says bashfully. "Horowitz is directing. It'll be announced Wednesday."

Lear! The others are gleeful. Lear—just think! He'll be perfect, won't he, he'll be the best ever!

"Well, I'll certainly be the oldest ever," Luther says.

The restaurant is almost empty. They slip into their coats, Luther knots his elegant muffler and leaves a lavish tip for all of them. "What's everyone up to this afternoon?" he asks.

"I? I will be napping," Coral announces. "Oh, and maybe I'll take a handful of those nice painkillers, to which I'm reputedly addicted. You know, this business of pretending to be other people all the time is quite all right. It gets harder to learn the lines, but at least there *are* lines. Pretending to be other people is fine. It's pretending to be oneself that's exhausting."

"Maybe you'll visit my father with me sometime," Emma says to her.

"Oh, I'd love to, Emma, dear. Let's be sure to arrange that."

"I don't really know what I'll do today," Duncan says. "I'm so rarely here, and there's always so much . . ."

"Why don't you come to the museum with me?" Luther says. "There's a Goya show. It's supposed to be splendid. And it's a beautiful day—we could stroll."

"Really?" Duncan says. "That would be wonderful. Anybody care to join us?"

They pause on the sidewalk, blinking in the wide blue dazzle.

"Good to see you all for a change," Roman says. "But I have a date to take my great-grandson to a movie. Keep in touch now, everybody, yes?"

"Your great-grandson!" Duncan says, and makes a little bow.

"Emma?" Luther says.

Duncan takes her arm. "Will you join us, Emma?"

But his voice comes from far away, from long ago. *Do you remember that day*, she thinks, *when we got together and we talked about that stupid book? We were all together, and it was a perfect day, a perfect fall day—do you remember?*

Cross Off and Move On

Adela, Bernice, and Charna, the youngest—all gone for a long time now, blurred into a flock sailing through memory, their long, thin legs streaming out beneath the fluffy domes of their mangy fur coats, their great beaky noses pointing the way.

They come to mind not so often. They come to mind only as often as does my mother, whose rancor toward them, my father's sisters, imbued them with a certain luster and has linked them to her permanently in the distant and shadowy arena of my childhood that now—given the obit in today's *Times* of violinist Morris Sandler—provides most of the space all four of them still occupy on this planet.

I was preparing to eat. I'd plunked an omelet onto a plate, sat down in front of it, folded the paper in such a way that I could maneuver my fork between my supper and my mouth and still read, and up fetched Cousin Morrie's picture, staring at me. Of course I didn't exactly recognize Morrie, and if I hadn't glanced at the photo again and been snagged by the small headline, I might have gone on for years assuming that my only known remaining relative was out there somewhere.

The tether snapped and I shot upward, wafting around for a moment outside of Earth's gravitational pull, then dropped heavily back down into my chair next to my supper, cracks branching violently through my equanimity, from which my family, such as it was, came seeping. I picked up the phone, I put it down, I picked it up, I put it down, I picked it up and dialed, and Jake answered on the first ring. "Yes?" he said wearily.

"Oh, Christ," I said, and hung up.

I dialed again and again he answered immediately. "My cousin died," I said.

"Your cousin?"

"Cousin Morrie. The violinist."

"Did I ever meet him?" Jake said.

"No," I said. "You never met him. Though you once saw a letter he—but *wait*!" My heart started to thud around clumsily, like a narcoleptic on a trampoline. "Why are we talking about *you*? This is about my *cousin*." I started to read: "'Morris Sandler, violin virtuoso, dies at sixty-six. Sandler was known as—'"

"'At sixty-six,'" Jake said. "At sixty-six, at ninety-three, at fourteen, at seventy-eight—at sixty-six what? Those numbers just aren't the point, are they."

"Have you been drinking?"

"I've been working. I'm at the lab. I'm sorry about your cousin. I didn't remember that you had one. You weren't close to him, were you?"

I held the receiver away from me and stared at it.

He sighed. "Listen, do you want me to come by?"

"No," I said, though I did want him to come by. Or I fiercely wanted him to come by, but only if he was going to be a slightly different person, a person with whom I would be a different person—a pleasant, benign, even-tempered person. "I'm sorry I called. Again. I'm sorry I called again."

"I wasn't being flippant," he said. "It just really suddenly struck me how primitive it is to measure the life of a human being by revolutions of moons and stars and planets. Anybody who still believes that our species is the apex of creation should—"

"How do you suggest we measure the life of a human being?" I said. "By weight? Would that be less primitive? By volume? By votes? By distance commuted? By lamentations? By beauty?"

He sighed again.

"Sorry," I said. I glanced around the room, the fading traces of Jake, still floating starkly against his absence. *I love you,* we still said to each other, but after a year and more of separation it seemed less and less likely that either of us would want him to move back in, and a vacuous, terminating, formal tone of apology clung to that word, *love.* It was like a yellow police tape at a crime scene. "Jake?"

"What?" he said. "What do you want me to do?"

I hung up again, tossed the omelet into the trash, drank up my wine to the accompaniment of the ringing phone, poured myself another glass, Friday night, why not, and flopped down on the couch with the newspaper as the ringing of the phone broke off.

Judging from the photo, Morrie, my only cousin, eventually came to look just like his mother, Adela. But as he seems to have had a wife at some point and was apparently a respected collector of original classical scores as well as a technically peerless musician, the resemblance—despite my mother's gloatingly doleful predictions—must not have demolished him entirely. He was obviously something of a mechanism—evidently he had amassed an enormous collection of train timetables in addition to the scores—as my mother always claimed, but that is unlikely to have been the consequence of having inherited his mother's nose.

As it happens, when I was five or six and Morrie was seventeen or eighteen, he still had blond curls and a flat face with an expression I interpreted as soulful—a plaintive, baffled look, as if someone had just snatched an ice cream cone from his hand, and I had private hopes that he might be an angel, though by the time I was able to formulate the thought, I had the sense to refrain from asking my friend Mary Margaret Brody, who could have told me for sure. In any event, at some point I commit the faux pas of announcing in the presence of both my mother and Aunt Adela that I will be marrying Morrie when the time is right. "Well, it's *your* life," my mother says, "but don't blame me when your children turn out feebleminded."

"Oh, that reminds me," my aunt says distractedly to my mother. "Did I forget to mention? Morrie is graduating summa."

My mother snorts. "You did not forget."

Later, when we are alone, my mother adds that in civilized parts of our country only criminals marry their cousins, and furthermore, she expects me to do better than someone in *that* family. Despite Adela's boasting, she says, despite the grades and the honors, Morrie has an exceptionally mediocre mind. It would be a miracle if he did *not* graduate summa from the tenth-rate college he is attending. The only reason he gets all those good grades in the first place is because he is able to memorize a freakish number of pointless facts. Naturally Adela finds this remarkable, as she can't even remember where she put her head.

"I expect you to outshine Morrie by far," my mother says. "You have much more to offer—*much* more. Your problem is that you don't apply yourself." Morrie's capacious but unnuanced memory was acquired from his father, who was so rigid himself that he toppled over and died at the age of forty, my mother tells me. Her impersonally disapproving gaze is directed, as she speaks, at a pair of stockings she is inspecting for runs. "And remember," she says, "Marry in haste, repent at leisure."

My aunts are the frequent topic of discourse when I visit my mother in her bedroom, where she sits in her big chair, her feet in a basin of water cloudy with salts and potions. The feet are lumpy, whorled, fish white, and riveting—trolls' feet, the toenails thick and yellow, mottled with blue. A fungus, she says. Blue and red graphs of her suffering run up and down the suety legs, which her hiked-up dressing gown exposes all the way to the thighs.

A slice of cucumber sits over each of my mother's closed eyes to reduce puffiness. And as she talks, I concentrate on spreading out my substance, making myself spongy to absorb the puffiness into myself, to absorb the pain radiating through her feet and legs and back. She works nights in the cloakroom of the club, standing all the time, and that's what accounts for the conspicuous veins that I find so fascinating but which, she explains to me, are disfiguring.

A familiar cold metal hand closes around my heart and squeezes: my mother is on her feet hour after hour, day after day, so that I will someday go to college. What an abundance of opportunities lies before me, for failure! Sitting on my mother's dressing table is a framed photo of a lovely girl. In this photo a heap of shining ringlets somewhat obscures the shape of the girl's head, but there are the distinctive, long, shiny-lidded eyes, their pale, nearly transparent disks of irises plausibly green though represented in black and white, with tiny, shocking dots at their centers. The expression, too, is well known to me, though the girl's suggests a mischievous rather than a malevolent irony.

It is hard to believe, but there is the evidence—always building to the same, ringing summation: a lack of advantages ate the lovely girl alive and emitted in her place someone shaped like a melting pyramid, on which is balanced a head—as wide and oval as my aunts' heads are long and oval—adorned at the ends with little frilly ears and topped now with a careful display of durable-looking, reddish curls, someone whose feet must sit in a basin.

I reach for my mother's hand and hold it tightly.

"What's the matter with *you*?" she says, but she allows

my hand to stay clasped around her fingers, even though it is clammy and disagreeable.

Flower to fruit to bare branch, sun to wan star—who am I to complain? The laws are the laws. I shake my head and clear a way for my answer. "Nothing."

———

"Your cousin Morrie was a beautiful child. My first thought when I saw him with Adela was to wonder if he wasn't adopted. Ah, well—no one in that family need worry about being loved for beauty alone," my mother says, impressing upon me the power of euphemism. In fact my aunts, with their coarse black hair, narrow faces, huge, vivid features, and long legs extending elegantly from their bell-shaped furs, look nothing like the other people in our little city—the Polacks and Litvaks, my mother calls them.

———

"What is this ludicrous obsession with aliens from outer space?" my mother says. "I am *not* taking you to *Women of the Prehistoric Planet,* so you can just forget about that." Aliens from outer space, she tells me, are, like Santa Claus, the invention of people too fey, too shallow, or too fearful to grapple with reality, or who stand to profit.

Still, I reason, surely there's no way to be 100 percent certain, especially because any aliens who came to our planet would take care to look as much like humans as possible, though it would be logical that they would get things just a bit wrong.

Also, it would be rash to judge the intentions and purposes

of aliens. There could be aliens among us who were sent only to observe, or even to help, not to meddle. Or—and these are the contingencies that seem most likely—aliens who escaped to the refuge of our planet from the terrors of their own or, conversely, who had been expelled, as a punishment, from the haven of their planet and condemned to the terrors of ours.

What is certain is that my aunts' house, which is draped in the shadows of the massive trees that surround it, has a stagey, provisional feel, as if it were an illusion produced by powerful, distant brainwaves, and I can't shake off the thought that the house dematerializes at night—its own form of sleep when its inhabitants are sleeping. I understand that the house is made of brick rather than brainwaves—it just *has* to be—but still, I brood about it: Hypothetically, what would the point of the illusion be? It would be . . . to get you to think that some particular thing was real, or else to get you to think that some particular thing was *not* real.

I once tried to describe to Mary Margaret, who had just gotten two great big, pretty, rabbity new front teeth and did not look entirely convincing herself, the way the house always appeared to be quivering in a twilight of its own and how you had to climb through shadows just to get through the door. "Do they have human sacrifices there?" she asked me, wide-eyed.

"Of course not!" I told her, looking frantically around for a receptacle, as I sometimes throw up when something unexpectedly upsets me. "My aunts would never do anything like that—they're so nice!"

But I always tingle with anticipation at the thought of the house, of parting the veiling shadows to explore its mysteri-

ous interior, and also because Aunt Charna might give me a
present when I next visit.

"Fortunately," my mother continues, "beauty is not the
only thing in life. Your Aunt Bernice and your Aunt Adela
are honest and hardworking. And we have to be grateful, because they've taken trouble over you. Your Aunt Charna has
some style, at least. That one wouldn't be half so homely if
only she'd do something about the nose!" She looks sharply
at me and then sighs.

Sometimes my mother takes me to the club where she works,
and even though it's exhaustingly dull to play in the cloakroom all day, I can bring my paper and colored pencils, and
there is a lurid appeal in the ambiguous suggestions of adult
life: the soft, luxurious coats and scarves, the interesting
muddy marks of huge shoes on the thick carpet when it's
been raining, the great big men who linger and talk with my
mother and who smell—and even look—like cigars, and the
pretty little basket that the men put change and sometimes
dollar bills into.

When we finally get home, my mother and I shake ourselves out and imitate the men we've seen that day, strutting
and braying, until I get the hiccups from laughing, and then
my mother makes me hot milk with honey in it so I can fall
asleep.

My mother heaps scorn on the men who come to the club,
but she heaps pity upon her sisters-in-law as if it could put

out a raging fire before it consumes her heart, though it seems
to add fuel instead. She argues their case over and over, taking
first the prosecution, then the defense. I understand this sort
of weighing and measuring, the adjustments and bartering,
very well. When I go to church with Mary Margaret, I pry
my mind open so that God's dragon breath will smelt the
impurities from my thoughts and I will be in an advantageous
position to ask that my mother be relieved of pain and live
until I'm so old that I don't care about a thing, even her death.

Her head is tilted back to keep the cucumber slices from slipping off her eyes. "More water, please," she says, flapping her
hand toward the electric kettle on the dresser. She huffs with
pleasure as I add hot water to the basin, and I feel in my own
feet the pain loosening its grip.

My aunts have undeniably beautiful legs—long, slender,
and shapely. Showgirl legs, my mother says—incongruous,
considering. She lifts the cucumber slices from her eyes and
hoists herself up a bit to take stock of mine. I note with
anxiety that the puffiness is not yet much reduced. "Good
heavens—why are you wearing that thing?" she says. "Isn't
that the same dress you were wearing yesterday? It makes you
look like an orphan!"

I hang my head. The dress is my favorite, a hand-me-
down from Mary Margaret, who is big for her age as well as
two years older but who spends time with me because, as she
says, she lives next door. Or because, as my mother says, she's
limited. I have been wearing the dress all week. Its length

and amplitude, in my opinion, cloak me in a penitential holiness, as though I were being led to the stake.

"I seem to remember that you were wearing it yesterday. Do I have to tell you again that's not nice? Go change. And be sure your underwear is clean, too, in case you're run over."

My mother is generally attentive to detail—my shoes are to be polished, my hair braided so tightly sometimes it hurts, my nails scrubbed, my handkerchief fresh, the clothes in my closet pressed and hung up or folded neatly, my bed made with square corners, but she has spent the last few days in her darkened room with a wet cloth over her eyes, which accounts for the lapse concerning my dress. When she is stricken with a migraine or when the phone rings and she must work extra at the club, either I am to fix my own supper and breakfast or else I am packed off to my aunts'.

"Best behavior!" my mother orders. "It's no easy thing, no matter what they say, to have a child underfoot, and I want you to make as little trouble for them as possible. No pestering, do not, under any circumstance, leave a ring around the tub, no prying, no personal questions, if your aunts offer you a gift, politely decline it—you have an unbecoming acquisitive streak and they can't afford to throw money away on foolish extravagances; moreover, we do *not* want to be beholden to them. Try not to get the hiccups, they're unattractive and could be interpreted as a bid for attention. Morrie has always been well behaved, and the coven will be brewing up reasons to find fault with me."

I protest—my aunts always say nice things about her, I tell my mother. "Hypocrites," she says.

———

My aunts live at a convenient distance from us, close enough
so that I can be parked with them whenever my mother is
indisposed or out late into the night but far enough away so
that we don't run into them at every turn, as my mother puts
it. My mother's high standards in pastry, however, sometimes
cause us and one or another of my aunts to collide at what my
mother says is the only acceptable bakery—or patisserie, as
my aunts call it—in our small city.

My mother keeps her back to the door as we sit at our
table in the bakery, but when one of my aunts happens to enter, I jump up, elated by this demonstration of destiny. "Aunt
Bernice!" I cry out.

"Hello, doll face," says my aunt. My mother dispenses
an icy smile toward which the impervious intruder returns a
sweet, vague wave, and I sit back down quietly, eyes lowered.
My mother rewards me absently with a little pat.

———

"Affected," my mother instructs me later. "Intolerably pretentious. Still, you have to be sorry for them. Their lives never
amounted to anything, they're too weak to fend for themselves, they have no resources of their own, and they don't
have the self-respect or drive to develop any. You're timid and
morbid yourself, so I hope you can at least feel some sympathy." She looks sternly at me and I nod. "A bad habit, timidity.
You have to learn to take the initiative and act decisively. But
it's no wonder those three are so helpless and wool-brained.
The mother was a tyrant. Be glad she died before you were

old enough to remember her. *Patisserie!* All you ever heard from that old witch was *Petersburg, Vienna, Krakow.* Petersburg, Vienna, Krakow, my hind end! They were smuggled out of some sewer in the Ukraine, the parents. They ate *slops.*"

Petersburg, I know, is *Saint* Petersburg, the place where people drank tea dispensed from the beautiful machine called a samovar, one of which I've marveled at in my aunts' house. Aunt Adela inherited it, as she's told me, from her own dear mother. "She brought that samovar all the way from Saint Petersburg. I don't know how she did it, the way they had to travel, poor things—the wagons, the boats, the vicious border guards . . ."

I look at my aunt. Where to begin? "Yes, darling," she says. "We mustn't dwell on it, but we have to be grateful. We have to be grateful."

The beloved item sits on a little marble-top table in the parlor, much the way the electric kettle sits on my mother's dresser, similarly a comfort and reminder of her own ancestral home, Great Britain. "My poor father's passage over . . . ," my mother says once, bleary with painkillers, and she trails off, dabbing at a tear.

"To heaven?" I ask after a few moments.

"What?" she says.

"To heaven?" I ask again.

She sits up and looks at me. "What are you doing here?" she says. "It's way past your bedtime."

What mustn't we dwell on? Well, everybody knows that, really: we mustn't dwell on what came before. Schoolmates and teachers have always asked me, for example, what my father does. Does?

I myself know better than to go around asking annoying questions. My mother does not tolerate such questions for an instant, not for one instant! And at school I feel perfectly entitled to answer questions of that sort as I see fit—my father has been a doctor in a leper colony, a bank robber, and a rodeo cowboy—which earns me a little reputation for unreliability. But by the time I'm nine or ten, I've learned to smooth over those awkward moments by just clamping my lips and walking off.

At my aunts' house, though, I plant myself conspicuously in front of an old, pinkish-gray framed photograph that hangs in the front stairwell. "Yes, darling," Aunt Bernice says. "That's our family. I'm the one on the left there, in the pinafore, and that's your Aunt Charna with the big bow in her hair, and your Aunt Adela is in the lovely lace dress. Those are our dear parents, and the littlest one, in the sailor suit, is your father." The six terrified-looking people dressed up in bizarre, old-fashioned clothing stare straight out, as if embarking on a perilous voyage. They all look exactly alike, including the little boy, my father.

"A *samovar*," my mother says. "For God's sake! I don't know why they don't sell that ruin of a house and all the vulgar old trash inside it and get themselves reasonable little places of their own where they could live independently, away from the spell of that harpy, and at least *dust*."

The dust in my aunts' house is the dust of transformations—

a languid, floating gauze that becomes sparklingly apparent when the rare light comes in through the tall windows. The gilded armchairs in the parlor are upholstered in dark velvet so worn on the seat and arms that the white muslin shows beneath, a ghost poised to emerge from within a dying body. The immense oriental rugs are worn almost white in places too, but as you study them the sleeping intricacies begin to surface in the weave.

When I am tired of drawing with the colored pencils I have brought, I mark off the hours, even the minutes, before I can return to my mother. The house is huge, and as many things as there are in it, it is still nearly empty. I go from room to room in the faint, gauzy sunlight, pausing to stare at some object or small piece of statuary until its transporting properties warm up. The ghosts flimmer in their chairs, the hieroglyphics rise in the rugs, the stopped gilt clocks and cracked ornaments begin to pulse with the living current of their memories, and a few filmy pictures, too faded to see clearly—streetcars and cafés and people in heavy, old-fashioned clothing hurrying along in a cold, twilit city—peel off into the sparkling dust.

Sometimes, when Aunt Charna is away on a trip with a person who has asked me to call him Uncle Benny or a person who has asked me to call him Uncle Solly, I sneak into her room and lie spread-eagle on her red satin bedcover that looks like a rumpled sea of blood, staring up at some splotches on the ceiling, which are friendly or unfriendly, depending.

In the room where I sleep there is a shallow fireplace. There are similar fireplaces in each of the bedrooms on the second and third floor—six in all. None of them work now, but Aunt Bernice says they all used to. Mine is the prettiest. The tiles are pinkish marble. Some of them are missing, and each blank patch where a tile is missing is like the blank patch left by a picture that shimmers for a moment in the transitional landscape of waking from a dream and then is gone.

I stroke the patches where the tiles once were, close my door, and descend one of the lordly mahogany staircases that march up and down the house, all the way between the attics and a vast, green warren of subterranean areas, thick with whirring pipes, that I've peeked into from time to time before scurrying back up into the house again. On one quick reconnaissance mission I glimpse a strange, tall table, covered with something fuzzy, sort of like blotting paper, that has channels along its edges and round drains in the corners.

"Is Morrie coming home soon?" I ask my aunts over and over when I visit. "Soon, darling," they say, but Morrie is always away now, at the conservatory, because he is to have a great future. He no longer looks like an angel, and when he finally does come to visit, he spends most of his time practicing, or playing duets with Aunt Bernice, though once in a while he can be persuaded to play cards with me.

"What is the fuzzy table in the basement for?" I ask him clandestinely, as he puts down yet another winning hand and rakes in yet another heap of matchsticks.

"The fuzzy table . . . ," Morrie says. "The fuzzy table. Oh, yes. Billiards." I search his face, but it's as blank as any good liar's. "Billiards was a game that wealthy people used to play."

"My other grandfather was rich," I cannot refrain from announcing to my mother when I get home.

"Have you been communing with the dead?" she says.

"Morrie told me."

"Well, Morrie's never wrong, is he. Yes, your grandfather on that side came over dirt poor like all the rest of them, made a lot of money in textiles, and then he lost it all in the Great Depression. He was poor and then he was rich and then he was poor again just in time to die, and those girls are living in the crumbs and ashes."

My mother says that when you hear Morrie play the violin you believe he really will have a great future, as an accountant.

One day my Aunt Bernice and my Aunt Adela bring me along on errands, and there in a shop window we're passing is a fluffy pink sweater that looks like cotton candy, just my size. "That would be adorable on you with your red hair," Aunt Bernice says, pausing.

On *me*? Joanie Hodnicki, the prettiest and meanest girl at school, has a similar sweater, but hers isn't even as good as this one.

"Would you like to try it on, doll face?"

My head starts to throb. It's true—I do have an acquisitive streak!

"Don't you like it, darling?"

It is impossible to speak, or move.

My aunts look at each other helplessly.

I close my eyes and feel myself sway as I imagine the delirious joy of squashing Joanie Hodnicki's face in.

"It's all right, darling," Aunt Bernice says, "You don't have to. Come along." I catch them exchanging glances again.

But what can I say when Aunt Charna returns from a trip with Uncle Benny or Uncle Solly carrying a gift for me? Because she can't just go back to where she was and return it! Once she brings me a big pad of delicious paper and some gorgeous crayon-like things, pastels, which I leave at the house for when I visit. And once she brings me a set of ten smooth, miniature square bottles filled with different colors of nail polish, *lacquers*, they're called—Sun and Jade and Leaf and Ruby and Midnight and Ocean and Flame and Amethyst and Dawn and Moon—which I successfully hide from my mother.

But the very first thing Aunt Charna ever brings me, when I am very little, is a lovely baby doll, and when Aunt Adela deposits me back home, I rush to show my mother. "She blinks," I say joyfully, waving the card that came in the box with my new doll. "And she *cries*."

My mother regards the doll dispassionately for a moment. How can she not be dazzled?

"And she can even wet herself!" I add pleadingly.

"Really," my mother says.

And so not only have I upset my mother, I have also humiliated a defenseless doll, who was given to me for safe-keeping.

My aunts have their suppers in the kitchen unless Aunt Charna is there with Uncle Benny or Uncle Solly and we eat in the dining room. We sit with our broth amid the silvery

clinking of our spoons against the chipped porcelain, and if
I squint, I can almost see the terrified old witch in the family
photograph—my own grandmother—at the head of the huge
table, hunched noisily over a dish of slops.

There are two pianos in the parlor. I don't play the piano.
My lack of musical talent is impressive, my mother has informed me, and lessons would only be a waste of money. This
is a shame, though, I explain solemnly to my aunts, who listen with raised eyebrows, because my mother says that those
of us who will not necessarily be able to rely on our looks
need to invest time and effort on cultivating our other assets.
My aunts look at one another, and then Aunt Charna puts
her hands over her face and lies back, her lazy, round laugh
rolling from her. My mother can be counted on to speak her
mind, she says, and Aunt Bernice and Aunt Adela titter a
bit, sadly.

Aunt Bernice plays a piece, making so much noise, it
sounds like she's playing both pianos at once. I inspect an
ornate gold clock that always says nine minutes after three
and contemplate the wonderful samovar—teakettle, I think,
severely—and before the piece finishes I still have all the
time in the world to watch a sated moth stagger along on one
of the silk curtains.

Sometimes I think I'll go mad, my mother says about one
thing or another. And sometimes I think *I'll* go mad, from
boredom—especially in my aunts' empty house, with its
ceaseless, nagging murmur of indecipherable allusions. When
I'm so bored I don't care whether I live or die, I go out in
back and consider the ravine.

The ravine is a great, jagged cleft in the earth, so clogged with vines and poison ivy and fallen trees and trash that you wouldn't know how to put a foot into it if you dared. Something lives down there with fur and bright eyes.

"Do they put dead bodies in the ravine?" I ask Morrie on his visit home. "Who?" he says, with that blank face.

———

"Those are shamrocks," Aunt Adela tells me as I peer at the happy little clovers on the teacup from which I'm drinking hot cocoa. "Shamrocks signify good luck in Ireland, where your mother's father came from." "Ireland?" I say, studying the shamrocks to affect indifference while a balloon of invisible information starts to fill up the room. "It was not Great Britain?"

"Ireland, Great Britain . . ." She shrugs. "I don't know where his people were from or why they stopped in Ireland. But that red hair of yours and your mother's probably came from Galicia, where her mother's family came from."

Galicia. I contemplate the beautiful name as it unfolds, disclosing delicate, prancing, caparisoned horses and the lovely princesses riding them whose undulating red hair reaches to the carpet of flowers beneath the hooves. "You could always tell the Jews from Galicia by their red hair," my aunt says dreamily.

"Oh, dear! Did you burn yourself, doll face?" she cries, jumping, herself, as my teacup shatters on the floor. "There, there, it's nothing, it's nothing."

"Galicia!" my mother says when I'm back home again, pouncing upon my cautious, squirming hint. "Absolute nonsense! What have those ninnies been telling you? My mother

was Hungarian. From somewhere near Budapest. Don't stand there with your mouth open, you'll swallow a fly. Budapest, the most sophisticated city in the world. Your grandmother was poor, but she was very beautiful and very refined. When she put down newspapers after she scrubbed the floor, she called them Polish carpets."

But I have more pressing worries than having gotten my aunts in trouble. Because it has struck me that if Mary Margaret finds out that my aunts and my mother are Jewish and—I suspect—that maybe I consequently am, too, she might not let me come to church with her any longer. I am not exactly allowed to go to church with Mary Margaret anyhow, so I have perfected a careful course between lying to my mother and disobeying her, and I join Mary Margaret when her frame of mind and my opportunities align.

In any case, my mother's main objections to my spending too much time with Mary Margaret seem to be that when he is not working his shift, her handsome father is often on the porch, drinking beer straight from the can, and that one of her many, much older brothers has been sent off to prison.

Still, it's not too hard to sidle next door to Mary Margaret's house, where nobody notices us especially amid all her relatives. And then sometimes Mary Margaret agrees to take me to church, though she won't let me get up to take communion with her because I'm not in a state of grace. I'm afraid to ask why not. I can guess. It's because I haven't washed well enough. But even if I've washed and washed, I don't protest, because I am more afraid of violating a rule in the lofty, solemn place full of God's echoes and perfume and fleeting colors than I am even of stepping on a crack in the sidewalk and breaking my mother's back.

Whether or not to tell Mary Margaret has been weighing on me for some time before I conclude that it is necessary, for the sake of my soul and hers, no matter what the consequences. So one day, after a wracking night, I hunt up Mary Margaret, to whisper my confession.

Mary Margaret whispers back: "I already knew it! My father calls you and your mother 'the Jews'!"

"Are my mother and my aunts and my cousin and I going to go to hell? Cross your heart!"

We stare at each other in consternation, and then she nods. "But maybe if I bring you to church with me enough, we can get your term reduced."

I get Aunt Bernice to clarify whether or not Jews believe in God, and she tells me that yes, absolutely, we Jews certainly believe in God, although strictly speaking, she herself doesn't and neither do Aunt Adela or Aunt Charna as far as she knows, though of course they all sometimes observe the High Holy Days together, and neither, she thinks, does my mother.

All right—so, you're walking around in a cloud of facts that are visible only to others. This has become evident to me. Your eyes blink, like a doll's, you can move your arms and legs, you can even cry or wet yourself, but you weren't born like a doll in a box, with a little card that says things about you, and if you want to know how it is that you arrived on this planet of ours, you can't just sit around blinking like a doll.

So, I begin to give detailed attention to my mother's bedroom and rummage when she's out. I find remarkably little of interest, except for a few ground-down lipsticks, a bottle behind her shoes, the colorless contents of which I identify confidently, after a puzzled sniff, as whisky, and small caches of money. These last have practical value at least, as Mary Margaret has been charging a small fee to take me to church with her, which seems reasonable enough now, considering.

I break into sweats whenever my mother emerges from her room frowning. But I am meticulous about covering my traces and circumspect in what I lift, and in time it becomes clear that she doesn't keep careful track. The secret activity produces an irresistible physical thrill, better than the stupid slides and swings in the playground, which I've long outgrown, better than horror movies on TV, better than poking a foot into the ravine at my aunts' house to see if the mud will swallow my ankle and suck me down into the vines and poison ivy and animals and dead bodies.

But it's as if my mother knows. Because around the time I enter high school, I always turn out to be wrong. I have gotten a spot on my skirt, or my hair is a mess, or my posture is deplorable, or—my mother says—I'm glowering. Nor do I do enough around the house, and I refuse, in general, to take responsibility.

That's true—but when I try to be useful, I wreck things! For instance, my mother has been distressed because the curtains are dingy and she can't afford new ones, so one Saturday, while she is working, I take them to the laundromat for a surprise, and out of the machine comes a big wad of shredded rags.

I throw up, of course. And when my mother gets home and sees them, she turns white and then red and then white again. She makes a phone call, puts me in the car, drives me to my aunts', reaches across me to open the car door, waits until I get out, and speeds off, without going in to say hello.

Aunt Bernice tactfully makes a pot of tea while I sit in the parlor, not crying—not crying—not crying even when she comes back with the tenderly painted little tray, the tea, the milk and sugar, and sits down not too far from me.

We sip our tea for a few minutes, and then Aunt Bernice says vaguely, "She was a beautiful woman. She might have expected more from life. My brother was a very charming person, but not very forceful. No doubt they both expected something very different. Your mother has had disappointments. And, frankly, darling, I suspect that the change is hard for her."

The change? Ah, yes. It's a fact. I used to look different. A bit like my mother. But now all that's left in me of her are my red hair and my unremarkable legs. Now I look like the other side of the family. I look like the little boy in the photograph, my father.

"Perhaps she feels it's the end of her life as a woman," my aunt says, gazing forlornly into her teacup.

All through the rest of the country, the rest of the world, people just a few years older than me are trying to learn to be kindly, rather than vicious, animals—letting their hair grow as long as it wants to grow, letting their clothes fall off, joining hands, considering matters of justice, hugging one another, smelling flowers, seeing visions. What clothes they do put on are brighter than any nation's flag. In our small city, where darkness and cold go on and on and most things smell and taste like lint, I groan with longing. The shadows of the freed young people flicker from the TV screen across my mother's impassive face until she summarily stands up and clicks off the set.

One Saturday my mother and I go to the bakery for a treat, and we sit at our favorite table. I am a bit smeary from eating my éclair with my hands, which is amusing my mother not one bit, and in walks Brucie Miller with his brother, Preston. "Hey, hi," Brucie says vaguely to me.

My hand is paralyzed in its reach for a napkin. "Oh, hi," I say, and look at the walls and the ceiling.

When we get home, my mother sits me down in the living room, which always means trouble. Why now? Did she see Mary Margaret sashay by in that tiny new skirt of hers?

"There's something we have to talk about," my mother says, and closes her eyes for a moment. "Pretty girls are not to be envied. Because when a boy sees a pretty girl, he does not see a real person. He sees a mirror of his own desires, and he falls in love with the mirror. Boys put a pretty girl on a pedestal. Do you know what I mean by that, 'on a pedestal'?"

"Obviously," I say.

"No need for truculence. A boy will do anything to get

the attention and admiration of a pretty girl, and then he courts and pursues her, and when she finally falls in love with him, he understands that she is not a mirror, and he runs as fast as he can. But girls who are not pretty are in an even worse situation. Boys believe that girls who are not pretty have only been put on earth as a poor compensation for what all boys believe the world owes them."

A hazy, swimming rectangle, filled like a battlefield with a distant clangor, inflates between me and my mother, though her large, staring face floats right in front of my eyes. Sweat begins to film my upper lip and under my arms, and I squeeze my clammy hands together as I hear my mother saying, "Boys know that girls who are not pretty are desperate for attention, and they congratulate themselves on the fact that those girls will do anything at all for what they can pretend to themselves is affection. So when a boy tells a girl who is not pretty that she *is* pretty or that he cares about her, she can make a fool of herself or not, as she chooses, but she believes him at her peril." And I am just about to be dissolved when I feel my aunts, with their strange, aliens' faces, which mine has come to resemble, marshal all their strength to cluster in the air behind me, a little phalanx facing my mother too, and I take a deep breath.

"What do you mean?" I say.

"That's what I mean," she says.

"What?"

"*That*. What I said." She gets up and goes into her room, closing the door loudly behind her.

"You must have wanted to get caught going through her things," Jake said to me many years later, when, in our early elation over the miracle that all the elements of the universe—a web of happenstance beyond calculation—had brought us together, we were tremulously passing back and forth to each other our biographies, containing all their apparently random data, as if they were precious archeological trophies that would sooner or later yield up, from some over-looked fold or crevice, a credible explanation, a key.

Maybe I did want to get caught—you could certainly make an argument for that, of the shallow psychological sort that generally contains some shred of accuracy—or maybe I did not. But in any event, I did get caught in her room going through a drawer, and by the time I did and the inevitable annihilating explosion occurred, I was sixteen and just out of high school and had grown far removed from Mary Margaret and God and any desire for salvation, and the money I had filched from my mother over the years and hoarded was enough, supplemented by hitchhiking, to take me nearly a thousand miles away, though no distance at all could be put between me and the unmistakable signifier of my weakness and cowardice, my pitiful, leechlike dependency on the life-blood of others, my congenital inadequacy: "I should have known that you were one of them," my mother said, "as soon as I saw that you were getting their nose."

It was owing to Jake that I eventually got work illustrating medical texts and that I studied enough biology and anatomy to be able to do so at all. When we met, I was taking a graduate degree in graphic art and working in bars and restaurants of various types. Since I'd arrived in New York I'd been a fry cook and a line cook and a waitress and a prep chef, and at the end of my shifts my overtaxed feet would swell with venom, which I would sometimes try to soak out.

But the night I met Jake I was tending bar at a place popular with young, stoned, Wall Street high rollers. It was a good and lucrative job, the best I'd ever had. The person who turned out to be Jake was sitting at the end of the bar under a feeble light, trying to read. He put a fifty down in front of him, and I poured him a draft and forgot all about him. My attention was on one of the regulars, whom I thought of, with loathing, as Mr. Perfect.

Mr. Perfect was the idol of our manager, Nelson, and he almost never came in without a shockingly gorgeous girl, rarely the same one twice. They would sit down at the bar, Mr. Perfect and the girl, and the predictable theatrics would start right up, so the moment he appeared I'd resign myself to a night of watching a wallet flirt with a price tag.

Mr. Perfect always ordered their drinks and awaited them and then criticized them a bit with a warm, genial manner as he suavely basked in the sunshine of his own power and his date's gorgeousness, a demonstration, obviously, intended for an audience. When the smugness index could go no higher, Mr. Perfect and his date would slip off their barstools and slide toward the door, merging as they went, leaving the rest of us adrift in their gamey hormonal wake to face our empty lives.

It was not Jake's presence in particular on that night that unmuzzled me, though it pleased him to think so, of course.

But had there been no witness to my degradation, no personable man reading at the end of the bar, I might have made it through the shift without opening my mouth.

In any case, I happened to be mixing a martini for Mr. Perfect's date as, right in front of me, Mr. Perfect was gazing into her eyes and scrounging under her sweater. "I'm sorry," he was saying, "but she leaves my mail in a mess to show that she's been working on it, she can't make a decent cup of coffee, she bites her nails disgustingly, she's awkward on the phone with clients, and this morning she actually put a call through while I was in a meeting with Rutherford." "You're such a perfectionist!" the date said. "I hate being a perfectionist," he said. "It's a character flaw, but I am a perfectionist so I had to fire her."

"Well, but maybe you didn't have to fire her because you're a perfectionist," I suggested. "Maybe you had to fire her because you're an asshole."

The warm and genial expression emptied from Mr. Perfect's face. It was the first time he had ever actually looked at me. "And you're fired, too," he said.

"You can't fire me," I said.

"*I* can fire you," said Nelson, unfolding out of some dimness. "You're fired, will you get out of here?"

"Gladly," I said, tossing my bar rag down as I extracted myself from behind the bar.

The guy at the end of the bar had looked up from his book and was staring in my direction with a lovestruck expression. I glanced over my shoulder, but no one was standing behind me. I glanced back at him. "You," he said. "You, will you go somewhere else and have a drink with me?"

"I'm filthy," I said. "Are you kidding? I'm disgusting. I'm covered with grease and brine. I'm sweating."

"So, will you go have a drink with me?" he said.

"No," I said. "I'm *filthy*."

"So will you go take a bath with me?" he said.

Over the years, it has dawned on me that people who have an immediate and deep response to each other also have an immediate and deep inkling of the dangers in store, and express significant warnings to each other that they then instantly forget for a very long time. "Look, I don't enjoy being an out-of-control furious maniac," I said. "If you think this is fun, that's a problem!"

"You won't be an out-of-control furious maniac if you hang out with *me*," he said. "I'll make you happy!"

"That's sort of an enraging thing to say," I said.

"Will you please get *out* of here!" Nelson said.

"Right away, boss," I said.

"Wait," Jake said. He grabbed the fifty he had put on the bar and produced a pen from his pocket. "Give me your number!"

In my confusion I hurriedly wrote my number on the fifty, then tried to snatch it away from him. "Hey, you're just going to spend that, and every ax murderer in town will be calling me."

Jake tore the bill in two and handed me the half without my number. "I'm broke," he said. "I'm a grad student. Have pity. I'll tape it up when we see each other, and we'll go spend it on a movie!"

"Will you get the fuck out of here *now*!" Nelson said.

"You don't have to ask me twice!" I said, and slammed out the door.

———————

Really, I believed that I had put my mother mostly out of my head during those years. But late one night, a little tipsy and with great trepidation, I called my childhood phone number. To my shock, the voice that answered was my mother's, and I realized that I had been waiting all that time to assemble a file of unimpeachable credentials before I contacted her. So pathetic. I might as well have been bringing a mauled mouse to my owner's door.

"You might have thought about me," she said. "You might have thought about the worry. I was sick with worry about you. I didn't even know if you were alive until Morrie told me he had heard from you, a year or two ago. It nearly killed me."

"I'm very sorry," I said evenly—though so intense was the flood of vengeful triumph engulfing me that later I couldn't remember how I came to find myself on the floor after I hung up the phone, though a few bruises suggested that I had simply lost consciousness for a moment and clonked myself against a table on the way down—"but you did say that you despised me, that I was a worthless waste of your life, that I was personally repulsive, whatever you meant by that—"

"Now, how could I ever have said anything like—"

"—that you knew the minute I was born that you should have given me to some poor stooge for adoption, that I smelled, that you never wanted to see me again, that you would have traded me for Morrie and a bag of compost any day—that sort of thing."

"I was disappointed in you," she said. "I said things I didn't necessarily mean."

"Ah, well then," I said.

"After all, you were no picnic. Are you in trouble?"

"Do you mean am I pregnant?"

"Well?" she said.

I was not pregnant, I told her. Nor was I in trouble of any kind. I had only called to tell her that, on the contrary, I was very well. I did not mention, of course, that I had graduated merely cum laude, but I did let it be understood that I had done well enough at a respected college (not one she respected, as it turned out) and had gone on to acquire a graduate degree, and that I was with a person she could hardly sniff at, someone who did work with deadly pathogens.

"'With'?" she said. "A *person*?" I heard her sit down abruptly.

Not to worry, as it happened the person I was with was a man, a very nice, flawlessly presentable man. A man who had stood by me, a man who had a high opinion of my abilities and character, a man who, in fact, actually liked—

"And is this paragon a doctor?"

I hesitated. "A researcher."

"I see. A researcher. And how long have you been with this researcher?"

"How long have we been living together?" I said. "A few years."

"'Living together'!" she said. "Is that how I brought you up?"

Most of my intimate involvements had lasted from about

midnight to about 2 A.M., as my mother might have expected of someone not on a pedestal, but the span of this particular liaison, with which I had intended to impress her, had obviously had the opposite effect, and after all this time I was still not equipped to endure her opprobrium. "Well," I said cheerfully, "'Marry in haste, repent at leisure.'"

She started to chortle but collected herself.

After that call, we spoke from time to time, cautiously. And then one afternoon she called to say that Aunt Bernice had died and as she'd expended so much effort on me she probably would have liked to know that I'd at least be willing to take a day off from all my important business to fly out and attend her funeral.

Jake insisted on coming with me, and as we entered the funeral home, I noticed that my grip on his arm was probably painful. Several shabby-looking old people were huddled together as if it were sleeting. Slowly it came to me that they were Aunt Adela, Aunt Charna, Uncle Benny, and my mother.

My shrunken and frail mother detached herself from the group and was walking toward me with great difficulty. "It's all right to cry," Jake said, putting his arm around me. "Go ahead and cry." "Fuck you," I yelped, and wiped my eyes and nose on my sleeve. My mother and I sort of made as if to hug but slipped off each other. "Mother, Jake," I was trying to say.

"Jake," she said, holding out her hands to him and radiating dewily like a young and beautiful woman, "thank you for taking such good care of my poor little girl."

"*Excuse* me?" I said, but they were embracing.

"Where's Morrie?" I asked.

"Tokyo," my mother said. "A concert, according to Adela. 'Impossible to cancel' if you please."

My mother had become quite hard of hearing. "This one's a mumbler, too," she said with distaste as the rabbi started the eulogy. "What's he saying?"

"That she was an exemplary person whom we all loved and looked up to very much."

"By God," my mother said loudly, "they're burying the wrong woman!"

Some years earlier I had tracked down Morrie's address—he was already famous—and I wrote him a letter. He organized it into questions, to which he responded with a numbered list:

According to records, our common grandmother 4 siblings, all stayed in Europe: 1 Auschwitz, 1 infant diphtheria, 2 Treblinka. Our common grandfather 7 siblings, all stayed in Europe: 1 Majdanek, 1 Chelmo, 1 unknown, 4 Auschwitz. My mother and your father 13 cousins: 2 Treblinka, 3 Auschwitz, 4 unknown, 4 Sobibor. You and I at least 5 cousins, all b. 1930–1944, all (known) Auschwitz. No known family survivors except our common grandparents. All four of our grandparents' parents, Auschwitz.

Grandfather probably Belarus or Lithuania. Grandmother Romania or the Ukraine. Nationalities depend on year in question, as borders fluctuated rapidly 19th and early 20th centuries. Primary language in any case Yiddish, which, no nationality.

Your father (my Uncle Joseph) went missing the month
before your birth. Attempts to trace him unsuccessful.

Morrie went on to say that it was very good to hear from
me, that his mother and her sisters always spoke of me with
affection and hope, and that he had fond memories of playing cards with me when I was a child and once taking me
to a movie about extraterrestrials that seemed to make a big
impression on me.

After the funeral service there was a little reception at my
aunts' house. My mother was sitting alone at one of the little marble-top tables, sipping something. She was staring
straight ahead, her face devoid of expression, as if she were
dreaming the house and everyone in it, the subdued hub-
bub around her, her life. It struck me that I myself would be
old before too long. I hesitated but remained standing and
then went over to say a few words to Aunt Charna and Uncle
Benny.

"I expected something immense," Jake said, gazing
around the parlor. "It's not really all that big."

Was it possible that he was actually a bit dim? "I was
smaller back then," I said with fastidious patience.

It looked miniaturized to me, too, of course, and only
seconds from shuddering into splinters. But it had almost
finished serving its purpose, anyhow. In the following few
years, Charna died, and then Adela and then my mother.
And now that Morrie is not around to remember them, my
aunts may finally be released from the house—the elegiac

murmuring of the carpets and chairs and billiards table and clocks, the unquiet sleep hovering over it, bringing dreams of the planet my grandparents came from, with its bloodstained ghetto walls, the pistol butts beating at the doors, its rhapsodic festivals of murder. Will I finally miss them, my aunts? I sit up on the couch, a bit drunkenly, to take note. Yes, off they go, my old allies, sailing right through the harsh, radiant shield at the edge of the universe, blending into darkness.

My mother invited us to stay with her the night after Bernice's funeral. Out of the question, of course, but Jake gallantly escorted her to her house, and when he got back to the hotel where we'd booked a room, he hugged me as if he'd just had an invigorating adventure. "Whatever else, your mother certainly has a lot of charm," he said.

"Charm?" I said. "What did she say to you? That she was grateful to you? For getting me on my feet? For improving my character? For staying with me despite—"

"Look, I know this is painful. I know that it's easier just to give over to resentment and to simplify the past by demonizing your mother rather than leaving yourself open to the stress of complex and ambiguous emotions. But you're an adult now. Your life is your own. Why not accept what a difficult life she had, and leave that all behind. Because even though it was necessary for you at one time, and gratifying, by now this resentment is obsolete, and it's just stunting you."

I got myself a separate room for the night, and after I called my mother in the morning to say good-bye, I met up with Jake for breakfast and I couldn't help mentioning to him that she had wished me better luck with him at least than she'd had with my father and said that he seemed like a decent man though a bit self-important, overly susceptible to flattery, and maybe not all that bright.

He took a quick breath in, and of course I was very, very ashamed of myself. "Your mother is as mean as a mace," he said.

"She's had a difficult life," I was evidently not too ashamed of myself to say.

———

When we finally got back home that night after being snowed in at the airport for hours, dealing with a ruptured carry-on bag, and sitting next to a sick baby in the lap of a sick mother who wore earphones that leaked tinny squawking during the whole flight, we had a long quarrel about the properties of vancomycin-resistant enterococci, which was something, frankly, Jake knew a lot more about than I did. By the time we'd used that up, we were completely exhausted, and we decided to take a couple of weeks off from our jobs to relax and get away from winter and just be together on our own.

And it was pure bliss, that holiday. One day, sitting in a nimbus of jasmine and orange blossoms in the gardens of an ancient palace while jaded-looking peacocks sauntered by, we considered the centuries of the kings and queens who had lived there and what it must have cost them to maintain so voluptuous and serene a refuge—the tyranny, oppression, and carnage entailed. But whatever the wars and lootings, they were long over, remembered by most of us, if at all, as a great number of names and dates that were easy to mix up.

And real as all those events had been, all that remained were the palace with its reflecting pools and galleries and gardens and peacocks, the carefree tourists like us, and of course the invisible consequences that would keep spooling out through eternity. I tilted my face up to receive the sun.

"What were you looking for in your mother's room?" Jake asked.

"I don't know," I said. "Nothing in particular."

"But, really—what were you looking for?"

"Oh, I don't know. Maybe a letter. A letter from my father, explaining why he had left. A love letter of sorts, I suppose."

"And what would the letter have said?" Jake asked.

He took my hand with such sweetness. I think I blushed, actually. Looking back, I suppose the future—its chilly plan for us—had cast a fleeting shadow over him and he was searching for what I would need him to say to me when the time came. But back then in that fragrant garden, I was aware only of the light coursing between our clasped hands and the sun's warmth on my face, with night idling where it was, half a world away.

Merge

What happened is that we got Merge . . . an operation that enables you to take mental objects [or concepts of some sort], already constructed, and make bigger mental objects out of them. That's Merge. As soon as you have that, you have an infinite variety of hierarchically structured expressions [and thoughts] available to you.

—Noam Chomsky

I know words. I have the best words.

—Donald Trump

1

Thundering down, a cataract from a high plateau, raising billows of dust, manes, tails, whinnies rippling like banners, a glamorous species, captive yes, but not entirely subdued, they—oh, no, a fellow in that ridiculous getup pops up from behind a rock and pulls out a—bink! That's enough, good-bye stupid old show, time for a cup of tea. Pulls out—bang bang bang. Yes, sensible Cordis decides, not a drink, time for a nice cup of tea.

The dog, a parting so-called gift from unfortunate Mrs. Munderson, peers at the blank screen, baffled, then paws at Cordis. Moppet is not glamorous, except in the most trivial sense; Moppet is cute. What does Moppet want? A treat? A tickle? A furlough?

Moppet wants whatever she can get. Moppet is a cornucopia of lacks, a prisoner—no, an overbred parasite, poor thing, entirely dependent on her hostess, Cordis.

You and I are stuck with each other, Cordis comments to Moppet subverbally as she puts the teakettle on to boil. "But winning ways have taken your kind far," she comforts aloud, "and soon they'll take you, as an individual, to the park. Assuming that boy ever shows up."

Park! Moppet's ears twitch. She sits, gazing meltingly up at Cordis. Her little tail thumps against the floor.

———

Cordis's mailbox is jammed. Keith has to pry the stuff out, and what wasn't already mashed and tattered is mashed and tattered now. All this paper! Cordis is singlehandedly keeping the post office alive.

Why can't she pay her bills online, why can't she look at catalogues online, why can't she get announcements online, like everyone else? He can easily teach her how. But the other day when he offered, she just waved a hand in her vague, languid, dotty way, and said, "Strange, but I prefer people." As if Keith preferred electrons.

All right, she's old, she can't be expected to understand things. But it's not as if digital communication is some outlandish new fad that she's going to outlast.

And to *what* might she prefer people? There's no indication that Cordis likes people at all! Nobody seems to call, she doesn't even use e-mail let alone social media, and as far as Keith knows, the only person who has ever come by is his . . . his what? His friend? His girlfriend? His . . . ? Anyhow, Celeste. But as Celeste's apartment is just down the hall, not a whole lot of preparation or anxiety would have been occasioned by those visits. And in any case, Celeste has been away for weeks now.

Really, Cordis's life would be so much better if she'd only acquire some rudimentary skills, skills that every kindergarten child is able to acquire. She's got a perfectly good computer, a recent hand-me-down from Celeste. And at least Keith has managed to convince her to use it for *something*. She could read the news, he'd cajoled; she could look at things—she could see anything there on that little screen: photos, magazines, movies, old TV shows—practically any rerun she wanted, going back to the dawn of time! Push a button, power over all re-creation! The goddess Cordis!

Predictably, she just stood there, an unsturdy tower, hands clasped tensely and eyebrows slightly raised, as if waiting for a child to conclude a tantrum, while he'd demonstrated, grinning and waving his arms like a used-car salesman. But obviously she'd taken something in, because since then he's caught her hunched over all kinds of weird stuff—clips of ancient comedy shows, *cowboy* movies of all things, nature documentaries . . . Just yesterday when he came up with the mail there were elephants behind her on Celeste's old screen, playfully squirting water at one another while some fool prattled on about them like a proud dad.

The damn catalogue he's lugging in must weigh five pounds. For this, a tree was torn limb from limb. Not that he, personally, much cares, but *Cordis* ought to. On the occasions Cordis deigns to speak to him, it's usually to air some peevish apocalyptic pronouncement—trees, habitats, resources, hurricanes, guns, polar bears, pollinators, this, that . . .

Get Cordis off these mailing lists, teach her how to find her catalogues and bills online—tasks of pleasing clarity to add to this ostensible job, a job as ridiculous as it is unremunerative and ill defined. For what does Cordis need a personal assistant? *My assistant will take care of it; I'll get my personal assistant right on that.* To whom would Cordis say such things?

During the weeks that Keith has been working for Cordis, he has brought in the mail, sorted her few bills, made some appointments with an acupuncturist, ferried her identical white shirts and black trousers to and from the laundry, and tried to organize a box of old photos—or rather, he started to try, but almost as soon as he lifted the lid she gently and wordlessly disengaged a snapshot from his hands, returned it to the box, replaced the lid, lifted the box back onto a high shelf, and went into the other room.

He's also walked the dog, picked up bottles of vodka and vast quantities of dog food, replaced a lost corkscrew, run out to the supermarket for a lemon and some teabags, to the pharmacy for ibuprofen . . . Four years at Princeton!

Humiliating, but for the moment it will have to do. And at least he can take satisfaction in doing Good. Yes, at least he can assist Cordis with navigating the vast seas of cultural ignorance where the elderly are cast adrift, each solitary on a decomposing life raft.

Celeste will see, when she gets back—which she is slated to do any time now—and returns to her pro bono tending of Cordis, how unselfish he's been, how responsible and thoughtful.

For a moment he basks in the halo of warmth throbbing out from his heart. Yes, Celeste will be delighted by the irreproachable way he's conducted himself. And by then he's sure to have snagged a *real* job, and his father will no doubt have dropped all the fuss about that borrowed money, too.

And anyhow, Celeste has promised to take him back in if he still hasn't found an apartment. In short, soon everything will be okay, all the wayward elements of his life will have snapped into place, making a seamless map for him to peruse and follow into his future.

In the elevator up to 6, Keith shuffles through the armload of mail: the giant catalogue, other junk to go immediately into the trash, bills . . . and hey, look, an envelope, a real envelope, addressed by hand! Who could be writing to Cordis? But—

Wait! The envelope is addressed to *him*—to him care of Cordis . . .

He slips it into his Italian calfskin messenger bag, muffling its faint black drumroll, just as Cordis opens the door of her apartment and he breaks into a sweat.

"Oh, *good*," she says, looking at him myopically over her glasses and reaching for the catalogue. "Moppet was becoming concerned."

What? He's not late! He checks his watch. "Oh, hey, sorry," he says.

"It's all the same to me," she says, leafing through the catalogue. "Speak to Moppet."

Five fucking minutes, big fucking deal, he could reasonably point out, plus given the condition of the subways, it's a miracle he made it at all. But—a template of genial maturity, mutinous impulses in check—he manages to effect a chuckle and says, "So, how are we all today, good?"

"Better would be impossible," Cordis says, without looking up from the catalogue. "And how are *we*?"

Keith suspects that Cordis is not entirely the loon she staunchly affects to be. Maybe, it occurs to him, her outlandish persona—like the large, strange, theatrical pieces of jewelry made apparently of rock and bone that she sometimes wears and that lie in artful heaps around her apartment—is designed to snare the attention so that she herself can be left in peace to wander through her realms of mental weirdness.

Cordis has slammed the catalogue shut and is staring at him severely, as if detecting his thoughts. *Look neutral,* he instructs himself, *you have nothing to hide,* but his heart is now racing in all directions, like the cockroaches last night when he got back to the apartment he's renting and turned on the light.

"It seems that feral horses revert to the behaviors of their wild ancestors, just as if they had never been domesticated," she says.

"Huh." His heart relaxes—those were not his thoughts at all! "Interesting."

"Well, that's what they're saying, anyhow. But tell me, *you've* just gotten out of college—"

"Okay . . . ," he concedes warily.

"So presumably you're familiar with what we believe these days. Do we consider ourselves to be domesticated? And if that's the case, do we think our brains have gotten smaller again?"

What *is* she talking about? "See, that's what your computer is for," he tells her. "You can look that up!"

"Because they say that domesticated animals have smaller brains than their wild progenitors."

"Yeah?" Keith says. "That's insane."

"I'll tell you what's insane," she says, holding the catalogue in front of him accusingly, as if it were irrefutable proof of his turpitude. "The whole thing." She heaves the immense shiny waste of wood pulp into the lovely basket she uses for trash. "Here you go," she says, and hands him Moppet's leash.

What could be less dignified than following this springy white puffball down the street like a courtier and placing its turds in a plastic bag? When Keith attempted to suggest to Cordis that the plastic bag part was beyond the scope of his office, she hardly bothered to respond. "Oh, please," she'd said. "When something that size shits, it's practically abstract."

"Chill for a minute, you," Keith instructs Moppet as he leans against some plutocrat's fancy, forbidding wrought iron gate to balance dog and self well enough to fish out the envelope that's been gestating there in the dark confines of his messenger bag. Very awkward—does this genteel block with its row of lovingly tended brownstones not place at intervals a bench to welcome the weary flaneur?

A *bench*! Ha! When has Keith last seen a bench in this town? Do people younger than he is even know what a bench is?

The senseless thought pellets ricochet off his brain as he struggles to open the envelope without either ripping its contents or strangling the dog: a bench! Some homeless person might *misunderstand*—some *homeless* person might feel entitled to *sit down*.

Keith loops the leash around his wrist, causing Moppet to leap, choking, in protest. But better an affronted dog than the wad of fur and gore he'd have to present to Cordis after a critical moment of inattention, and the envelope seems to spring open, leaving a vicious little cut on his finger—an incriminating streak of blood, a tiny crime scene marking a mortal struggle with a piece of paper.

The handwritten address on the envelope, now smeared and dripping, is shocking. The letters, formed in black ink, are as personal as fingerprints—more intimate than any previous contact he's had with Celeste, though one might have thought that there could hardly be anything more intimate than their previous contact. Unnerving, he reflects, to be so familiar with someone's body and yet never to have seen her handwriting.

And yet, how would you come to see a person's handwriting? Nobody has written anything by hand for, like, hundreds of years. Except maybe a check. But a letter? He might as well be clutching an illuminated manuscript! Hm, it's not a letter, it's a postcard . . .

And in the same ink, the same curves and lines, precise and delicate as the tracing of a heartbeat or a brainwave, meaning unfurls:

My assignment is completed. I've moved on. This is the view from my window. On a good day you can see the pretty carousel, but usually it rains. Mostly, the people here eat a crude kind of chicken pie and a tuberous thing that looks like a rutabaga.

WATCH THE SHADOW ON THE DIAL
TIME IS PASSING

Hm. So much for meaning. What *is* the matter with these two, Cordis and Celeste! Could it be the water in the building? Well, sure—not for nothing does he always bring his own.

But what does she mean, she's moved on? That project of hers is finished, she says; it's time for her to come *back* . . .

This seems to be some kind of cryptic rebuke, does it not? What is it this girl is trying to get across to him, and why doesn't she just *say* it! He *knew*—even before he opened the envelope he knew it would contain a rebuke.

Though actually it's her own fault that she's so disappointed in him. He never lied to her, he never tried to pass himself off as some kind of saint. But it's impossible for her to think that there might be anybody alive who wouldn't share her overheated notions (evidence to the contrary) about—

about absolutely everything, so she's shocked when that supposition turns out to be erroneous. She made certain assumptions about him and his attitudes, which he failed to correct promptly. But how could he have corrected those mistaken assumptions of hers promptly? How is that *his* fault? He didn't even realize she was making them!

Calm down, he urges himself. Why is he so agitated? It's as if every little thing these days activates some new, anxiety-producing source he's tapped into!

He turns the postcard over, but there's no explanatory text, no view from any window—no colorful depiction of a carousel or even of anything that looks like a rutabaga. In fact, there's no image at all—it's just a generic blank postcard of the sort you can get at any post office. Where could she have sent it from? He peers at the envelope—the postmark is indistinct, and the stamp is inscrutable.

The card is unsigned, of course—a trite move to alarm or intimidate or assert domination, though Keith understood, as he was obviously meant to understand, the instant he saw the envelope in the stack of innocent bills and flyers that it was from Celeste. Who else would know to address something to him at Cordis's?

Except for the National Security Agency, come to think of it, though the NSA has other things on its mind. Or at least it ought to. And except for maybe a couple of his father's underlings, or his father's accountant, Sam. And possibly except for some regional law enforcement units, too. Theoretically, anybody can find anybody these days, even if you toss your phone into the sea, which Keith did, and follow the reams of advice you can find about disappearing from the grid. They know you've looked for that advice. They know *that* you've looked for it, they know *how* you've looked for it, from where and exactly when. These days a person cannot simply disappear.

Moppet is jumping up and down on all fours, looking like an automated cleaning implement gone awry, and glaring at Keith. Why this glare? Why this bark?

Sure, sure, everything is his fault. He glances at the postcard again and then stuffs it back into his messenger bag.

He relinquishes his comfortable leaning position against the gate, gives Moppet's leash some more play, and ambles on, whistling carelessly, a suave movie star from days of yore. There were probably security cameras beaming down on the fence anyhow, squadrons of armed goons poised to burst out of the air and gun him down. Self-defense, they'd claim later over his bullet-riddled body; the dog was going for the throat.

Keith crumples the envelope with its darkening blood-stain and lobs it into a pile of trash; Moppet flings herself indiscriminately at every curiosity. A water bug will do. She's managed to find one just about her size. She barks happily, but it doesn't want to play with a dog any more than Keith does, and scoots away. Oh, well, resilient temperament or short attention span, she's on to the next thing. Oops, it's a pit bull—Keith scoops her up before she is swallowed, and now everyone's glaring at him—Moppet, the pit bull, the pit bull's owner, whose giant arms are enrobed with pulsing prison tattoos. "Heh, excuse," Keith says, making a getaway with his handful of yipping fluff and a bright smile.

2

He can hardly remember his life before Celeste. Actually it was only a few months ago that he met her, but since then, things have taken some pretty surprising turns.

And to be honest, he does owe Moppet, because he never would have looked twice at the, what, rather soft-looking girl with the abstracted expression and the badly cut hair falling over her big, round glasses if the tiny dog she was walking had not lunged at a Great Dane, entangling Keith in her leash.

"Okay, hold still," the girl had said.

"No worries," he said. The dog quivered while she held it, unwinding. "But while you've got me here, do you happen to know of any, like, real estate place in the neighborhood that deals with rentals? I mean, cheap, relatively?"

She did, in fact, but the directions were involved. "Say again?" he asked.

"So, use your phone," she said.

"No phone," he said. "No phone, no laptop—I was staying at my dad's while I look for an apartment, but he's a pretty horrible guy, actually, and I couldn't deal with him anymore."

"Logic?" she said.

"Oh, sure. What it is, is I left kind of hurriedly and he's pretty furious, so all my—"

"Whatever you say," she said. "None of my business."

She wasn't his type at all. Of course he wasn't such an idiot as to have a type, he reminded himself, but she certainly wasn't the type of any guys he knew. And detaining her had been far from his mind—he really was looking for an apartment in the area, though there were probably none available, she assured him as they walked.

It was the vestiges of obsolete grandeur that had attracted him to the neighborhood, really—the few old, incongruously swanky brownstones, for instance, like the one whose fence he had just been propping himself up on, that remained standing among all the dilapidated remains of the last building boom. If he had to sacrifice his father's apartment, he might as well retrench to someplace where at least it *looked* like a person could lead a reasonable life.

It was a beautiful day, he remembers, unseasonably warm— not that there actually were seasons any longer, as the girl observed rather ritually—so they'd lingered outside the Realtor's for a bit, basking in the worry-evaporating sunshine while the dog appraised the ankles of passersby.

"Listen, thanks for your help. I really appreciate it," he said.

Actually, he *did* appreciate it. Everything had been sliding around, roughing him up since he'd left his father's apartment so precipitately, and her air of certainty was bracing—she just seemed to have been put together more on purpose than other people. Anyhow, more on purpose than he'd been.

She turned away—exercising no wiles, and yet he felt a slight tearing sensation. "Can I at least get you a coffee?" he'd said to his own surprise, indicating an attractive café across the street. He glanced around—not that some guy from school would just happen to be walking by and observe this!

"No thanks," she said. "Moppet? Come on, Moppet." But the dog was stubbornly inspecting Keith's boot. "Moppet? Oh, well, coffee, why not."

"I guess I don't seem charming enough to be a psychopath, huh," he said.

"Cheer up," she said. "Sure you do. It's just I could really use some caffeine, so I'll take my chances."

Her name was Celeste, he learned; she was four or five years older than he was, though she sort of looked like an eight-year-old, brooding about what flavor of ice cream cone to get. She worked at something she called a humanitarian crisis management center, it seemed that she lived alone, she referred to no boyfriend or girlfriend, and she was walking the dog, now curled up in her lap, for someone who lived down the hall.

Her office would be sending her to Europe soon, she told him. The project would take about a month, and then she'd be given some time off. "During which I'll probably just sleep for a few weeks. It's pretty tiring work."

"Wow, a job in Europe," he said. "That sounds great. I don't suppose they need someone else?"

"I'm kind of trained? But they always need volunteers. You could definitely be plugged in someplace if you want to be a volunteer."

A volunteer! The exact opposite of what he meant.

But still, a volunteer job in Europe would address both his lodging and his father issues. And how long could it take to rise up in the ranks? "So where's this gig taking you, exactly?"

"Slovakia," she said.

Slovakia? That was what she meant by *Europe?* "Guess I'd just get in the way," he said.

"Could be," she agreed.

"Well, listen," he said. "If you hear of any jobs or any apartments here in the city, would you let me know? I'm pretty desperate."

She looked at him intently, as if she were adding up columns of figures. "Well, okay," she said after a moment, "I'll ask around. Give me your number in case I do hear of something. Oh, right—no phone. So, how do I get in touch with you?"

"What about—well, could you meet me here on, say, Thursday?"

Again she considered him.

What was going on with her, he'd wondered—girls generally jumped at the chance to see him!

She shrugged. "Okay, why not. I'll be walking the dog, anyhow."

3

His father had decreed: yes, Keith could take a year off before law school or business school. But only on condition that he move out. He was to get his own apartment and a job. *You're twenty-two years old. By the—*

Yes, yes, by the time his father was twenty-two, et cetera, et cetera . . . Had his father memorized some script?

Had he studied his lines at schools for rich thugs? Well, come to think of it, sure—at the same schools he'd gotten Keith into . . .

But this same man—the CEO of SynthAquat Solutions, the lord of irrigation and crops, who could divert rivers and move lakes, who could flood fields for thousands of acres or leave them to be scorched, who could squeeze a stone and make coins come clattering out of it—this very same man was unable to grasp certain elementary facts: these days positions were not just sitting there the way they used to be, waiting to be filled by personable young men like Keith; these days apartments were not just sitting there, waiting to welcome personable young men like Keith.

With the best will in the world but without a phone call from his father whose name was the key to all locks, how was Keith supposed to manage? And his capricious father was suddenly not about to pick up the phone.

"I'm sick of doing every single fucking thing for you." His father had looked at him as if he had only just noticed his presence. "Get you into this school, get you into that school, send you skiing here, send you sailing there. Just like that hopeless fucking train wreck from whose dainty loins you sprang. What are you going to do if some girl gets me to leave everything to her, huh? Happens, you know—it happens. When you're old and gaga. That's what they do, unsheathe their little talons, tie you up, drug you, sweet-talk your crooked lawyers into changing the will—how are you going to survive then, kiddo? Are you a pancake? Could I have produced a pancake? Now, take some initiative for once, just go on out there, do what you have to do, and don't clutter up my life with your, 'Gee, Dad'"—and his father had produced a cruel, treble whine—"'how do I do this, Dad, how do I do that?'"

But to rent even the filthiest burrow it turned out that it was necessary to show one's bank and employment records, to present affidavits, letters, proofs of eternal solvency—in fact, to demonstrate that a year's worth of rent money was sitting around in one's bank account!

He was a pancake? He took no initiative? The great man didn't want to be bothered? Fine. There would be plenty of future opportunities (Keith had been thinking, as he extracted a check from one of the checkbooks his father kept in the top right-hand drawer of the desk in his home office) for father-pleasing displays of acumen, innovation, leadership, public speaking—all that sort of thing. Taking things in hand like this was at least an indisputable display of initiative. Who could say he was not going out there and doing what needed to be done?

How could he have anticipated that Sam, his father's private accountant, would notice a discrepancy so slight as ten thousand dollars in one of his father's zillions of accounts, or that he would question the signature, so zealously studied, so faithfully reproduced, on check #8703? Or that his father would fail to recognize the spirit of playful creativity exemplified by Keith's minor—and temporary, obviously!—redistribution of funds?

He certainly hadn't spent all that money yet, but the longer he searched for a place to live, no matter how frugal he was, the less of it was left. And therefore the less likely that any landlord would accept him. It was one of those paradoxes, he later observed to Celeste, that philosophers study.

4

Without his electronics he was a virtual amputee. Or more like someone who had awakened nearly blind and nearly deaf. The fine mesh of chats, e-mails, postings, and so on that had buoyed him along shriveled away overnight. He strained to receive the world's breeding influx, which had sustained him as plankton sustains a whale, but it was— nowhere!

One good thing at least—not only could his father not find him, Tish couldn't find him, either. Tish was a nice girl, he'd meant every word he'd said to her, he was sorry he'd gotten tired of looking at her, but that nonstop texting! It had been driving him nuts.

For a while, featureless clouds of static filled his ears, his lungs, hung in front of his eyes. How strange it was to find himself in this barren expanse! But just as the other senses are said to intensify when vision goes, in the absence of his accustomed interface the bare, sharp vividness of things had begun to assail him; he felt like he was being etched. How great coffee was! How gross that gunk around the baseboards was! One morning he realized he was staring at his hand, marveling, as if it belonged to a stranger, to an alien creature. And was that him, sitting in the café with this Celeste person? Each time he met up with her, the moment would come when, to his amazement, he asked to see her again.

An irony had begun to bother him, he eventually mused to her. People were drawn to what they thought of as him, but it wasn't really him, he now understood. What people were drawn to was an aggregation of qualities he'd had little hand in making or choosing, that he himself might not, as he was noticing, have a lot of respect for: his appearance, his reasonably good manners, his passable education, his general range of circumstantial, historical, evolutionary, whatever, ornaments. But he had a persistent sensation—and didn't she agree?—that there was some rubbery little nub through which those more superficial qualities were routed—his *self*?

"I don't know," Celeste said. "All that stuff is pretty inalienable. I mean, it's all you, qua person, isn't it? But obviously you're in process. It's interesting. Maybe you're just turning into you. Or maybe you're changing course. Or maybe you want to change course, or maybe you've got to change course because there's an obstacle in your path or because something's not right about the path."

Not right? Definitely something was not right! Like, maybe he was on his way to prison? Maybe he was a congenital pancake?

"Anyhow," she said, "one thing about all those ornaments

that fate hung on you—they give you the luxury to make some choices."

Luxury! He was a guy who didn't even have his own apartment!

It was after their seventh date—or meeting, as Celeste called those pleasant occasions—that she invited him to move in with her. Well, not move in, exactly, but to bunk with her until he found a place of his own.

A haven, the cozy little apartment at the back of the building, with Celeste curled up, late, late, overlapping him. Was this happiness? he wondered. He felt like a pioneer; he was expanding outward toward his own confines—toward his infinitely elastic confines. Exciting. Scary . . .

It was soothing to stroke her soft hair; after tumults of love, their breathing phased into serene alignment.

Beyond the apartment's walls, in the night sky of his closed eyes, little lights charted the streets and broad avenues, the apartments and clubs of late revelers, the tall towers, where five or six guys he knew, guys only a few years ahead of him, would be toiling, even at this hour, in their big chairs, the vast windows of their offices overlooking the city, overlooking the planet with its mines and wells, its fields and great waterways, as they steered Earth's course by the graphs and instruments of their predecessors' devising into the hidden future.

Hidden also from those guys was Celeste's wild ocean of sheets, calming again now, and bleached lunar white by the film of night light that slipped in at the window, where he and she floated, safe.

. . . *like a boat,* Celeste murmured, as they moved off on
slow waves of sleep, farther and farther from shore.

5

The second postcard arrives in Cordis's mailbox about a week
later, also in an envelope, which he tucks firmly away until
he's gotten out on the street with Moppet. Moppet's little
toenails, or whatever they're called, skitter on the hall tiles in
her haste to be out the door. His heart pounds.

Moppet makes for the sad little patch of earth in front of
the building where a scrawny tree grows, no thanks to her,
and pees as he tears open the envelope:

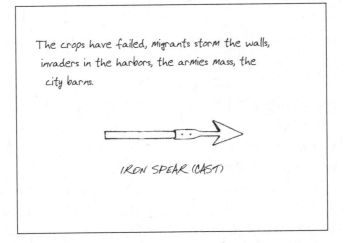

The crops have failed, migrants storm the walls,
invaders in the harbors, the armies mass, the
city barns.

IRON SPEAR (CAST)

And what's that supposed to mean, "the city barns?" Oh,
wait—it must be "burns." The city burns.

6

During the days, while Celeste was at her office, Keith continued to send out his threadbare CVs and look for a job. But the magic name he shares with his father was suddenly a liability. Because why, the personnel department at one prosperity mill, and then the next, must have wondered, had the dad not supplied an introduction? No calls back. Not one.

———

"Okay, so your father won't help you out," Celeste had said. "But that doesn't mean he's a criminal."

"He's got really, really a lot of money, though. He's got *extra* money. He's got mountains of it, he's famous for money. He's SAS."

"*SAS? SynthAquat Solutions?* The people who poisoned all that water in Malaysia?"

Oops—maybe that wasn't exactly how he should have explained his father to Celeste. And anyhow, it wasn't the point. "Well, they do plenty of other stuff, too," he protested.

"SynthAquat Solutions! No offense meant, but your father actually *is* a criminal."

Tears stung his eyes—yes, his criminal father! How was he ever going to recover from the way his father spoke to him that day? He'd heard his father unleash his wrath on employees, on wives, but he'd never imagined what that would really feel like. It still sometimes flashed through his body like pain.

And in fact, if his good luck hadn't bumped him into Celeste . . .

A terrible thought struck him. "Listen," he said. "I can stay in your apartment while you're gone, right?"

"Excuse me? That is, obviously I had to rent my apartment out. I mean, sorry, but to people who can pay something? I've already set it up through SpacesCadet. People are scheduled to be in and out the whole time I'll be gone."

She was leaving . . . she was really leaving. And bad enough that she was leaving, but the apartment would be, in a sense, leaving with her!

"Sorry," Celeste said again. "But it's not for all that long. And if you haven't found a place by the time I'm back, I guess you can stay again. This isn't news, is it?"

"News? I mean, you have to do what you have to do. But you know, I've *got* to get a job—I've got to get a job right *now*, *any* job."

She patted him and let a little interval of silence cushion his panic. "Well, listen, you know the lady whose dog I walk?"

"That lady you work for down the hall?"

"Cordis? I don't work for Cordis."

"Well, but you walk her dog."

"She's my friend. She hates to go out, so I walk her dog."

"Why did she get a dog if she hates to go out?" He seemed to be tumbling through the air, clawing at it for a hold.

"She didn't get a dog. The dog was Mrs. Munderson's, from 4B. But she forgets to eat."

"Mrs. Munderson forgets to eat if she's got a dog?" Oh, why couldn't something other than this be happening? Out of all the possibilities, why would life have bothered to invent *this*?

"No, *Cordis* forgets to eat. Look, I'm really sorry. So I bring her stuff sometimes. And help her out with her bills, that kind of thing."

"You pay that lady's *bills?*"

"No, I keep track of them. Sometimes she just stacks them up and forgets about them. She's had some hard times. Her husband disappeared almost twenty years ago. And she used to run a great bookstore, one of the very last in the city, but obviously that had to close sooner or later. Anyhow, it would be good if she had someone to check up on her and walk the dog and stuff while I'm away."

"What, *me?*"

"Why not?"

"Like—what, like a personal assistant?"

Celeste looked at him, then shook her head briefly, as if she'd gotten water in an ear. "Okay, personal assistant, whatever."

PA for the old weirdo down the hall? Well, but at least it would be something sufficiently chest-thumping to put on that pathetic CV of his: Personal Assistant. *Personal Assistant to Cordis Whoever.*

"Hey, but what's this story with the husband? Did he go off with the lady in 4B, or what?"

"Mrs. Munderson? Why would he have gone off with Mrs. Munderson? They took Mrs. Munderson away."

And that was how Keith had learned about Ernst Friedlander and Friedlander's quest to study the origin of language.

"The origin of language?" This, too, was confusing. "Didn't it just come in the kit? Tool-using, bipedalism, language?"

Other animals were bipedal, Celeste reminded him, and *lots* of other animals, as it turned out, used tools. And obviously other animals were capable of communicating with members of their own species—in some cases even further, apparently beyond the taxonomic divides humans had worked out for them.

And although some animals were capable of figuring out how to use some human symbols to communicate with humans (though oddly humans couldn't much figure out how to use animal techniques to communicate with animals), evidently no species but their own—humans, modern humans, *Homo sapiens sapiens* (an awkward classification necessitated by some initial miscalculation)—shared an innate capacity for using a flexible system of abstractions that was amenable to complex elaborations. No other species had a capacity for fitting together elements—thought entities, so to speak, mental units that could be expressed as words or phrases—to make larger expressible thought entities.

For example, Celeste said, two of these thoughtish/speechish units could be linked together—via this system, grammar!—to create a new, more precise, and more complex unit, which itself could generate other, even more complex units, all governed by the laws inherent to that spectacular innate capacity.

"Like noun 'Cordis' and verb 'remembers.' 'Cordis remembers.' Or 'Cordis remembers her husband.' 'Cordis remembers her husband although he disappeared twenty years ago.' 'Cordis remembers her husband, who disappeared twenty years ago, although she forgets to eat the cupcake on the counter.'

"So we can formulate a lot of content—ideas, relationships between ideas, nuanced relationships between ideas, all that—with these little things, words. Grammar's, like, an operating system?"

"Sounds valid," he conceded.

But Celeste's eyes were shining. "Of all the different humans and humanish beings they keep finding, it seems like we're the only ones who were ever able to do this! And the most amazing thing is that even though various kinds of humans were around for maybe almost two million years, this language thing really only kicked in probably around one hundred thousand years ago, or even less."

Only? Even? Those were big numbers Celeste was tossing around—100,000, 2 million . . . hard to tell the difference between them if you weren't some kind of expert. "So, if we weren't talking for that first one million, nine hundred thousand years, how did anybody know what was going on?" Keith asked. "And what were we doing? Just kind of goofing around with the dinosaurs?"

"Dinosaurs died off about *sixty* million years ago?" Celeste reminded him. "First grade? There was a comet, or maybe they just became extinct because they were really big?"

"My dad's really big," Keith said gloomily, "but he's not extinct."

No, it never would have occurred to him to wonder if that fateful leash hadn't looped his destiny to Celeste— *language* . . . what exactly was it, and how did it happen?

Celeste shrugged. "Some people think it was just business as usual—mutation, adaptation, selection, mutation, adaptation, selection, a slow continuity kind of thing, for hundreds of thousands of years. But other people think it happened incredibly fast, within about forty thousand years. And that this capacity that made it possible—this built-in capacity for the operation that lets us merge expressible things into other expressible things to make more and more complex expressible things—appeared in an instant! Which makes complete sense, even though it could not be more bizarre. One tiny molecular irregularity in one tiny fetus, in a very small population of humans somewhere in Africa! One instant! A universe-altering mutation!"

"But what about . . . ," he began, but ran aground.

"What about the other stuff? The stuff we can't manage to think?"

"Yeah," he said. "Or . . . well, I mean, yeah."

"Uh-huh, that's a problem. Actually, Friedlander was pretty interested in that. In his opinion, language developed as a way for us to deceive ourselves into believing that we understand things, so then we can just go ahead and do stuff that's more ruthless than what any other animal does. According to him, we can formulate like a fraction of what's inside our heads and that what's inside our heads is mostly . . . drainage, basically, sloshing around, that doesn't have too much to do with what's actually out there . . ."

They looked at each other, and vague shapes, like amoebas, rose, morphed, blended, and faded between them. "But at least it's all ours," she said. "It's the main unique thing we've got. It's our gift."

So, Celeste brought him down the hall to meet Cordis.

"That kind of money is a joke," Keith said when they were alone again. "How can anyone work for that kind of money?"

"It's not a joke to Cordis," Celeste had said.

7

Celeste, it turned out, knew a fair amount about this Friedlander who had disappeared. Keith was surprised to learn that she had grown up in the very apartment, the somewhat cramped paradise, from which he was soon to be expelled, down the hall from Ernst and Cordis Friedlander.

Her mother, she told him, had been a good friend of theirs, and the three of them often sat around one apartment or the other, laughing and talking till all hours, over delicious dinners and glass after glass of wine, and often she had hung out with them, too.

Friedlander went on long expeditions, and it was always a party when he came back, always a party when he was around. He was very good-looking, rangy and graceful like Cordis—they were an intense, matched set. His face was a constant play of expressions, as Celeste remembered, but he didn't much say what he was thinking about. He had black, black eyes and a lot of black hair. His clothes were sometimes frayed. He didn't care at all. And he didn't need to; he set the rules—no rules, mostly, and he seemed to change shape, alternately filling up a lot of space and slipping between spaces. His laugh was loud and sudden, and a little dangerous. He was even taller than Cordis.

And Cordis was different back then, Celeste said—way different, always doing things, always cheerful. The three of them, Cordis and Friedlander and her mother, would sometimes just bundle her up in the middle of the night, or it seemed like the middle of the night, and embark on some impromptu adventure. She vaguely recalls a carnival, or a fair, with brightly painted rides, a merry-go-round with the most beautiful horses imaginable.

Sometimes Friedlander brought things back from his expeditions, strange and marvelous salvagings. The little thing she wore around her neck? It was a piece of glass he'd found in some ancient forgotten city buried beneath another ancient forgotten city buried beneath another ancient forgotten city. He gave it to her because it was the exact color of her eyes, he'd said . . .

Yes? Keith peered at Celeste's eyes. Well, okay, but so were a lot of things . . .

While Friedlander traveled, she was saying, Cordis always stayed put to take care of the bookshop, and Celeste had hazy memories of the suspended sweetness of those long stretches, the gauzy, slightly melancholy quality of early-spring light—playing cards with her mother and Cordis. At those times she was like a grown-up woman herself, waiting. She was only about eight when he disappeared, evidently for good.

Keith had frowned with lofty sympathy and put an arm

around her. "Well, at least he was spared getting old and decrepit."

She'd looked at him for a moment. "Right," she said.

Apparently he'd committed another faux pas.

8

Sometimes Cordis seems to Keith like that vaporous picture in Celeste's mind—far away, even when she's right in front of him, down a tunnel of time, she and the serious little girl in big, goggly glasses and the little girl's mother, each studying a hand of cards, all three dissolving as they wait for something that isn't going to happen—just three blurs, indistinct stains of their future selves left on a memory that isn't even really his.

It's Friedlander, though, the one absent even from this scene, who has left the most vivid impression: tall, laughing Friedlander, as curious and lawless as . . . as a monkey, thinks Keith, clambering around ruins, plucking from the debris shiny things with which to charm. Obviously all three of them were obsessed with him, the two women and the little girl, sitting there, waiting and waiting. Those three and who knows how many others.

It's irritating to spend so much time in a place that's draped in this guy's absence. Maybe a few well-angled questions to Cordis would let in some fresh air to dispel the guy's clingy remnants. But he can't just ask Cordis a lot of questions. Or, rather, he can't manage to. It almost seems that she can detect a question as it forms itself in his brain, and she swerves like a toreador, before he's even found the words.

However, thanks to the Internet's admittedly not completely reliable but nonetheless far-ranging knowledge, he has been able to fill in what Celeste has told him with what information and misinformation is out there.

Back in the day, he's read, Friedlander's grandfather made a fortune manufacturing steel. And while Friedlander's father, brothers, and sister devoted themselves single-mindedly to amplifying the fortune, staying just inside the limit of the law—usually (like Keith's own father) by getting the law's limit altered to fit their needs—Friedlander dabbled in a series of eccentric, quasi-scholarly enterprises, as only the useless child of a wealthy family can. A wealthy, generous, intelligent, kindhearted, tolerant, appreciative family, that is . . .

He's read, also, about Friedlander's purported habits of shutting himself up alone for months at a time, of swimming in ice-cold water, of encoding his charts and records in notations that look more like arcane architectural exercises than academic findings. And he's read that Friedlander is said to have been involved in the discovery of a prehistoric site, now vanished again, on some island somewhere between India and Myanmar, where he had hoped to find evidence supporting his hypotheses.

During a botched attempt at an initial excavation, Friedlander along with his teammates, Jack Brisbane and Helmut Ogilvy, disappeared. Rumors and speculation cited the militias that roamed the region, uncontacted tribes, coastal flooding, an earthquake . . . But whatever actual knowledge might have existed twenty years ago about that episode has by now dissipated into a haze of fabrications and fantasies and misunderstandings.

In any event, it seems that nobody has been able to locate the site that lured the three dreamers east.

What clowns. Whatever the three crackpots (or "maverick archeologists," they're sometimes called) were up to (looting, essentially, is what it sounds like), it appears that in no way did they take reasonable precautions, either in regard to their own safety or to avoid damaging precious clues—for many millennia hidden away under the earth's custody—concerning the development of the chattering species.

From the evidence of the few relevant newspaper articles he was able to find, Keith has also gathered that Friedlander's evolving ideas about human speech, once provisionally regarded as original—his opaque musings concerning some convoluted, indirect relationship between language, thought, and power—were ultimately dismissed outright by serious linguists.

In fact, serious linguists (of which there seem to be a stupefying variety—psycholinguists, sociolinguists, neurolinguists, paralinguists, archeolinguists, biolinguists, computational linguists, morphologists, phonologists, and structural linguists, to name just a few) as well as philosophers, archeologists, ethnobotanists, anthropologists, biologists, geneticists, and primatologists of many sorts, have continued to close ranks against Friedlander, denying him entry even now into their rarified company.

9

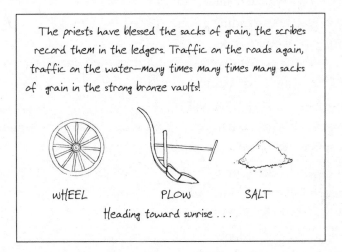

The priests have blessed the sacks of grain, the scribes record them in the ledgers. Traffic on the roads again, traffic on the water—many times many times many sacks of grain in the strong bronze vaults!

WHEEL   PLOW   SALT

Heading toward sunrise . . .

It's Celeste's handwriting, that's for sure, but it's strangely shaky.

10

It's dark. Or maybe she hasn't opened her eyes. Has she opened her eyes? She must have opened them, because when she tries to open them she can't. She feels around for a light switch—last night there was one near her, just above her flat little pillow. Was that last night? Oddly, her bed seems to have moved. It's now blocking the door—nowhere near the light switch. But that cannot be true, so her eyes must not be open.

She needs some water badly. She struggles to open her

eyes, and now she succeeds. But her bed is outside in the corridor, with all those women padding by, speaking whatever it is they speak, their heads wrapped in brightly colored lengths of cloth, their long, beautiful bare feet slapping softly on the linoleum floor.

But the women are gone, and now she's burning, burning up—she must have water. She wills her eyes to open, really to open, and she finds that she's alone, back inside the room. But where is that dim light coming from? Because now there's no window.

Let me wake up, she prays, *please, please let me wake up.* But she cannot.

Many hours later—a day or so later?—her eyes do open, her bed is where it ought to be, maybe eight feet from the door, and a grimy morning light is coming in from the high little window. She's slippery with sweat. Her fever seems down, but her skin feels sore and whatever that stuff is inside her skull seems to have swelled up.

There's a sink in the room. She could drink from the tap . . . The tap! What is she, crazy? If she can just hold out until she gets downstairs . . .

Several days earlier, when she arrived, there was a man, presumably the owner, or a manager, seated at what seemed to be a school desk in the bare space that serves as the lobby. If she can get some clothes on, maybe she can make it down the stairs and get him to understand that she needs water. She tries to sit, but she's a marionette whose strings have been severed, and she can't hoist herself up.

No one's going to help you, she thinks. *No one. You're a migrant.*

One day, maybe her fourth or fifth in this place, she wakes up hungry, very, very hungry, and she feels as though she has shed a heavy, suffocating hide. The loveliness in things has never been so apparent—the loveliness of the bedstead's raw wood and of the mattress ticking exposed by the soaked, twisted sheets, the loveliness of the rough walls and the dented metal doorknob, the loveliness—the effervescent freshness—of the light, spreading out from the high window. Each material is radiant with the soul of itself.

She raises her hands to catch the loveliness of the air as it runs sparkling through her fingers.

There's an open, half-filled bottle of water by the bed. It must have been brought during the night by the young woman she dreamed, thought she dreamed, maybe the manager's wife.

Later she'll get up from bed to wash at the sink, but now she'll finish the bottle of water. A collection of empty bottles sits on the floor near the small wood table by her bed, the only feature of the room aside from the bed and a wardrobe and the sink and a toilet.

Heading east—an impulse too furtive to formulate into an idea, let alone a plan. But that was what she'd found herself doing, heading east. After all, she was already across the ocean and she had a few free weeks. They'd known she wasn't one of the best, she thinks with sorrow, they'd known she would need time to recover if she was to have any use left in her.

Spontaneous Structures of Authority Among Refugee Populations. She'd thought she was prepared, but it was only during one instant and then another that she could take in what was in front of her, things that ought to be impossible—the miles of cardboard and plastic, rotting garbage, sewage, the clashes at the margins and in the adjacent towns, clashes in the bus and train stations . . . every port sealed. Each child a little bundle of twigs, not one thing for anyone to do except wait, and hope for food, the women huddled for safety in ineffectual little bands . . .

Of course she'd known what to expect—she was trained as an Observer, she was trained to take testimony, she'd seen it before. But if what she observed was real, how could *she* be real?

Money moves across the globe at the speed of thought, at the speed of poison in water, but when will these people be allowed outside the wire enclosures?

The giant machines crushing the plastic roofs and cardboard walls, plowing them into the mud—she can still see it! She can still hear it! It sounds like your own bones. The rain pelts down, and the people look on, silently, at the plastic and tin and splintered boards soaking into the mud.

Now they can go. Now they *have* to go. *Now.*

But go where? *Not here. Not here. Not here.*

———

Time to get out of bed, time to wash at the sink.

But that is apparently not possible.

Look—someone has left something for her beside the bed! A fresh bottle of water and something roundish, with a slightly bumpy, mottled, copper-colored surface. Could it be? Yes—the covering peels right off, disclosing a globe composed of tiny, iridescent segments. Juice bursts out as she bites into it, and an intoxicating fragrance flares into the room like daybreak. Ah, thank heaven!

She feels the nutrients going here and there in her body, patching things, easing things. But that's enough, a couple of bites—she doesn't have the strength to finish it. Really, she would love to be at home—she has a home! And that's what she would like best of all. Home. Does that boy miss her? "Miss"—miss—what does that mean? Is there a little hole in him where she was?

Unfortunately, she can't seem to scrape him off her mind, entirely. Or, not her mind, exactly, but her something. In fact, on the contrary, he is more present to her now, here, than he was when she was back there. *Home.* His molecules have mingled with hers in some creepy way, with her mental molecules. That's what happens when you get to know somebody, even slightly—or even if you just catch a glimpse of someone on the street, or even if you just hear about someone! If you try to pull them out of your mind, you make a raggy little hole.

Once someone enters your mind, no matter where he is you can dream about him—someone can dream about *you*, whether you've given permission or not . . . If someone dreams about you, does it keep you alive?

Sure she wanted him to be someone else, or at least sort of someone else. Pretty much everyone wants everyone else to be at least sort of someone else, don't they?

And evidently he himself wants to be sort of someone

else. He's trying. He deserves credit for trying. His effort is exhausting, she can feel it—but she must not try to help him. She must not try to hamper or influence . . .

Oh, she'd been blinded—worse, she'd been enchanted—by what even *he* knew was the trashy, low-grade pixie dust of undeserved advantages. And she'd been even *more* enchanted by her own—quite possibly entirely unfounded—conviction that there was a noble something or other beneath all that, struggling to exist! And now she was giving him extra credit because he was *trying*!

She was going to help him become a human being? Classic narcissistic self-serving fantasy!

He had tried to tell her how incomplete he is—she'd refused to understand. He'd had to force her to understand, the very night before she left! Though of course he couldn't admit he was admitting what he was admitting.

"You *stole* from your father?" she'd said, incredulous.

"I *borrowed*. Anyhow, I didn't ask to be born—he started it, so he's kind of obliged to keep it going, don't you think? I mean, you could say he owes me my upkeep, couldn't you, morally, until I've finished grad school anyhow."

"You happen to be one of the few people on the planet your father doesn't owe anything to!"

"Right. Well, that's actually my point, really. You can't exactly call what I did stealing, because my father shouldn't really have all that money—he's ruthless, he's cruel, he doesn't care how he treats anyone, he's a criminal, you said so yourself."

"Great, now you both get to be criminals. What do you think, this is some kind of Robin Hood situation? Robin Hood stole from the rich and gave to the *poor*."

"I'm the poor," he'd objected.

"You actually *are* a psychopath!" she'd said.

"Look, you're entitled to your low opinion of me, and I understand why you'd feel this way, but it's fundamentally unfair. Or it's only temporarily fair. I just haven't been in a position recently to exercise my potential for decency much. But listen, by the time you come back, I'll . . ."

Her stare seemed to have stopped his words. "By the time I come back you'll what?" she'd said.

He'd been sitting at the edge of the bed with his head in his hands. After a moment he spoke indistinctly. "I'll what—good question. Yeah, what am I saying."

His father had destroyed whole harvests and swaths of villages—his father had sent people scurrying across the face of the earth, but this kid's problem was that he'd been more or less kicked out of the guy's apartment?

She'd moved to the couch, where she'd spent the night. In the morning he packed his things and she gave him a pitiful little good-bye kiss—a little dried flake of affection—and then they were both on their way.

Even in her sleep she feels her way along the surface of the day's banalities for some rough patch that indicates something hidden, something buried, a sealed door behind which, if she is alert, she will be able to hear Friedlander's heartbeat. Even in her sleep she watches for the ephemeral shapes, rising above the dark horizon like iridescent soap bubbles, of the first words to be uttered on the planet.

She's all sticky with the juice of that fruit, but it has given her strength. Soon she'll be able to get up, walk around, get on another bus to somewhere else. Somewhere that wants her to be there. It's as if she's attached to a cord that's being reeled in from far away, no matter how much she wants to go home.

Across from the bed where she lies, the pale light on the wall is turning rosy. That thing in her head begins again, and now the wall runs red. Illness has entered, beating its dirty wings as it devours the soul in the light, the wood, the doorknob.

The women are pattering down the corridor in their bare feet, and time is passing rapidly in one direction or another. She has some postcards left. Where are they? The information hangs just outside her head. She lies still, to let it float in. Yes, the postcards are sitting right on the little table. If the quiet woman returns with water, Celeste can give her one to mail.

11

The cows are cattle, the goats are a herd, the grasses are a field. Over in the valley the people stay put. Dogs prowl, dogs watch and eat meat from their hands.

Pot   Spindle

Boat   Thread

Harp   Brick

When can I come home? Please send for me soon.

There's no doodle on this one—just a sticky sort of splotch.

———————

This city is crazy expensive! His money—his borrowed money—is disappearing fast. But his hours for Cordis, even given Moppet's episodic requirements, are flexible, so he's been able to fit some additional wage earning around them. And he's had to.

Any old job, people say. But what do they mean, "any old job?" It's no joke, it turns out, to flip burgers or bus tables or stock shelves or move furniture, let alone clean toilets.

Sorry, it's not working out, he's been told more than once.

You bet it's not working out! That stuff is incredibly boring, and it's also, weirdly, hard to do it right. Who can stand doing it? And for what? You could hardly call that money—it's no more than he's making as Cordis's PA!

And now he's tired all the time. Has he ever been tired before?

Not this kind of tired. He's been tired after skiing, he's been tired after sailing, he's been tired after excellent nights out. But with that kind of tired, he always had a feeling of accomplishment. This kind of tired comes with nothing good at all, no feeling of accomplishment, just the dread of how tired he'll be again tomorrow. The dread of the endless exhausting, boring chores he has to perform to keep himself alive. Now walking Moppet is the high point of his day.

———————

He no longer has the sensation that he's being hunted by his father's people, but neither does he hope any longer for

a message from any of them—some indication that his father has forgiven him. It's more as if he's been forgotten—
abandoned . . .

"Heard anything from Celeste?" he asks Cordis—
casually, he hopes.

Cordis has not. Funny he should ask just now—she tried
Celeste's number just this morning, but wherever Celeste is,
she's apparently not getting phone service.

———

Cordis lets him use Celeste's old laptop, so every once in a
while he checks his e-mail from her IP address, but he checks
it without hope. And thanks to the bounce back he put on it
right before he left his father's apartment (au revoir, love you
guys!), his former friends have given up. All he gets is spam.

———

Always, now, as he takes in Cordis's mail or goes in and out
with Moppet, there are new people—people around his age,
he judges, and even younger, certainly the youngest people
in the building by far—squealing behind Celeste's door or
tumbling around in the hall, glorying in his loss. New renters, every few days—who-knows-who's.

He himself is a who-knows-who, renting by the week
through the filthy little real estate office Celeste directed him
to the first time they met. As he watches the agents smugly
scrolling through the possibilities online, his head comes
near exploding with rage. He could do so much better if he
could only deal with the matter online himself.

But he can't deal with it online himself—thanks to his father, he's powerless; he's been forced to kill his online identity, he's only a body now, a ghost.

And the apartments that fit into the budget of the pittance he has left aren't a tenth as nice as Celeste's. When he turns on the kitchen lights, there are those roaches again—the cockroaches scattering like a hallucination.

Kitchen! He's lucky if he finds a place with a hot plate. All night long he's awakened by scavengers crashing through the garbage out front. And if one more bug bites him, he'll fall into shreds.

Maybe it's this heat—there hasn't been heat like this ever in the summer, people keep saying. The streets are clogged with ambulances and fire trucks. Just yesterday there was shouting and then smoke was filling the apartment where he's staying for a few days. Flames were shooting out the window of the building next door.

By the time the fire trucks got through, the entire top story of the building was charred. And when he got to Cordis's place an ambulance was blocking the entrance. They were carrying an old woman out on a stretcher. Cordis! he thought for a sickening second—but no, it was just one of the other old ladies who were still left in the building.

So many sirens! Have there been so many sirens all along?

––––––

Where is Celeste! Where is Celeste! She was due back weeks ago. Why doesn't she just come back? How could he possibly send for her? He doesn't know where she is!

They had really a nice dinner together the night before she left. He had bought a bottle of wine, not the greatest, maybe, but wine. He made spaghetti. He washed and dried the dishes, and then they tumbled around together, listening to music.

She lay with her head in his lap, and they mused, he remembers, about language. Language—what does it clarify, what does it obscure? Is a person a person without it? Is all that stuff inside your head there whether you have language or not? Do chimps have all that stuff inside their heads? Is the stuff you can figure out how to say the same as the stuff inside your head? Is the stuff inside your head the same as the stuff inside the world? And when you say something, why is there always extra stuff inside your head that doesn't fit into the words at all?

He made little braids in her hair. An idyll! He was free, elated, exhilarated, as if he had run away from home.

"You did run away from home," she said.

And then—stupidly, stupidly!—he confided the precise circumstances in which he had.

He hadn't exactly intended to? But as he spoke, two things happened: he felt a great burden sliding up out of his body, a burden he hadn't known he was hauling around with him—and almost right at the same time he heard the story of borrowing that money in his own voice, just as she would have been hearing it. Yes, he had studied his father's signature. Yes, he had gone into his father's private things and violated his father's trust.

How could it have happened so fast? One moment he was one person, an instant later he was another. Was he only a set of reflections—pancake-like specters with shifting features—staring at one another from ghostly mirrors? He was choked with indignation and sorrow, as though his good qualities had been stripped from him by a rough hand, like medals.

12

Moppet stretches out in Cordis's lap to watch the animal shows. Sometimes she leaps to her paws and barks with what seems to be an anguished longing. It's the old cowboy movies that seem to affect her most—especially the shots of cattle. Something about those cows . . .

She barks and barks, but the cows pay no attention. Poor lonely thing—she must miss Mrs. Munderson so much.

Cordis often leaves a movie playing for Moppet to watch on her own, but she has to admit that she likes the animal shows, herself. All these years, with no screen of any sort whatsoever, and now this wealth of animals for herself and Moppet. Well, she does have to thank her dog walker for that.

Though she still isn't accustomed to having this diabolical machine around. *Obviously* she knew—probably before the dog walker, Keith, was born—that it's possible to read the news on a computer. But why would she want to do that? Even the sight of Celeste's laptop sitting there quietly all closed up is a bit ghoulish. All that idiocy, all that violence, all that confusion coursing through its tiny electronic veins—whether you happen to be looking at it or not. Bang bang bang. Bang bang bang. Why bother to have four walls around you?

It's irritating to be considered a curiosity, even by someone as young as Keith, and it's hard for Cordis not to be impatient with the boy. At first, whenever Cordis tried talking to him, things seemed to contort somewhere between her brain and her larynx. Was that what she meant? she wondered as she spoke.

Even to herself she seemed like the crazy old lady he believed himself to be gawking at. And when it was his turn to talk, she couldn't understand him any better than he had seemed to understand her—it was all a bit wrong, as if she'd left her head out in the rain.

At first she was mystified that a woman like darling Celeste would have taken up with that kid. Though he is very attractive, she recognizes, in a sort of formulaic way. What would Ernst have made of the boy? Oh, dear—she can just imagine!

But heaven knows, Celeste has never been able to resist a challenge. And clearly, it's a seller's market in this city for men these days.

In any event, he's been looking tired—exhausted, really. She knows that he's taken on a few other, very undemanding little jobs, but that can't entirely account for his fatigue, let alone his haunted look. He seems to be engaged in some profound internal struggle. Her heart goes out to him, at least partway.

Just yesterday he seemed so tired that she offered to let him take a nap while she went out with Moppet, but to her surprise, he drew himself up gallantly, gave her a wan, reassuring little smile, and soldiered on to the door, clutching Moppet and her leash.

Hopeless, the poor boy, really. The pity in the little smiles he sometimes wrings from her must be all too discernable.

––––––––––

An odd consequence of having him around is that she finds herself thinking about Ernst all the time. Not that there was ever a time when she didn't think about Ernst—after the early, annihilating pain, the clock simply stopped, and he has been with her at every moment, though muffled—neither receding nor clamoring.

But it's as if this clueless young person has let time slip in through the door of the apartment, turning her well and truly old in an instant, turning to dust all the beautiful things Ernst brought back—the remarkable carvings and adornments—letting light and air decompose all her precious photographs of the two of them, the boy's fingerprints on their decades together. Leaving Ernst stranded, far, far—just about twenty years—away.

Oh, shouldn't Celeste be back by now? Celeste is a grown woman, she doesn't need somebody fussing over her—but still, Cordis hasn't been able to restrain herself from trying Celeste's number a few times recently.

Because Celeste is still the infant in Miriam's arms, the child down the hall, the small visitor perched in an armchair, chomping her way seriously through a cookie as they all discussed the metaphysical matters that preoccupy children: Does the color we call blue look the same to all of us? If God created the world, who created God? How do I know that you're real? Or that I am? Ernst had almost as much an appetite for Celeste's questions as she had for his answers . . .

Cordis has a sudden memory of a caressing summer evening. They all—she and Ernst and Miriam and Celeste—went out to some grimy, festive little fair for children. Celeste would have been scarcely two. They stood in line for the merry-go-round, and Celeste gazed, intent and puzzled. Suddenly she turned around to them. "Horsey!" she shouted, and they had laughed, elated as if at a major scientific discovery. "Horsey!" they echoed.

The tool that doesn't work, Ernst called language. Or at least it worked to further comprehension and communication in only the most restricted ways. An extremely plastic faculty, amenable to many uses, but it developed to serve the pressing demands of malice, vengefulness, and greed—humanity's most consistent attributes—providing individuals with the means, through lies, boasts, propaganda, fearmongering, advertising, derision, and outright threats, to subjugate others. If that's what you want to call intelligence, go right ahead, he said; how proud we were to be able to articulate our misconceptions, our limited, distorted views and visions!

Conversation? She had reminded him—poetry? By-products, he said. In his view, language was mainly for bullies.

The other day she went out for the first time in weeks, and just outside the door of Celeste's apartment was a heap of old food wrappers and some discarded drug paraphernalia. It looked like a murder scene.

Out on the street the people seemed to be emanations from a grainy silent movie of long ago. Is she getting sick? What will happen to poor Moppet if they come for her, too?

<hr />

She pours herself a glass of vodka and stands at the window, as if she were watching for Ernst and Celeste approaching, hand in hand. Apparently it has suddenly become late. Or maybe there was to have been a big storm today. Or an eclipse. She's forgotten, but the sky is an occluded gray . . .

Is she waiting for a great catastrophe, or only the minor personal one?

13

The sun is at its zenith when Celeste gets off the bus, but it's surprisingly mild. And the trail through the jungle glides along underfoot.

Apparently no humans have hunted or harmed the animals here, because they observe Celeste placidly as they go about their business. Large striped and spotted cats flow down from their perches in trees and pad by, close enough to touch. Their jewel eyes gleam through the foliage. Bright parrots flash into the sky.

How nice it would be to sit down on one of these big, gnarled roots and watch the animals, but there's no time to spare. In fact, it's already late afternoon when she arrives at the council. She seems to be the last, but that's probably all right, as the others seem in no great hurry to start up.

A preoccupied-looking orangutan is brachiating nervously through the vine-laden trees encircling the clearing, but all the other hominids are just milling around or lounging on the rocks that appear to have been designated for them, grooming one another, as Celeste slips quietly into the circle and assumes her seat.

She notes with interest that there is a significant representation of humans. She spots a few she recognizes, mostly among the younger members of the crowd. There are some mild-mannered Neanderthals, she sees, and an absolutely adorable *Homo floresiensis*. Oh! And there's a rather alarming *Homo heidelbergensis*! She's glad she hasn't been seated next to him!

There are so many others, though, much older and looking rather the worse for wear—all kinds of australopithecines, she conjectures. All in all, there's an absolutely bewildering variety. Who knew?

Naturally chimps and bonobos have turned out for the event, as well as gorillas, and things must be starting up, because an anticipatory rustling and gibbering ripples through the crowd. The participants frown with concentration—empty conveyances form in their heads and line up, preparing to receive their cargo of mental plasma. *Word*, Celeste thinks, encouraging—*word*, and the *Homo floresiensis* scowls, fluttering a hairy hand, as if batting away a swarm of pests.

One of the chimps is dragging out some large placards. They keep getting stuck on a root, but eventually the chimp gets them propped up against a tree in a stack, in such a way that everyone can see the top one clearly.

Rays of the setting sun come slashing through the vegetation—it's impossible to make out what is written on the placard. Celeste squints. It just looks like gibberish.

A couple of other chimps run up and fuss with the placard—oh, it was upside down. And although the handwriting is a bit shaky, now Celeste can see that it says, INTRODUCING.

One of the chimps pulls the placard away with a flourish, as if it were a flash card, to reveal the next one, on which is written, OUR.

The maneuver is repeated, and the third card is revealed: FIRST.

And then—the final card: SPEAKER!!!!!!!!!

There's another expectant ripple through the crowd, as a man appears and takes his place at the podium, smiling and nodding magisterially. He looks familiar to Celeste . . . She knows the face from somewhere or other . . .

Oh, yes, that's Keith's father, isn't it? He clears his throat and glances irritably around. One of the Neanderthals is wandering around the assembly holding a glass of water. Keith's father clears his throat again, snatches at the glass of water, opens his mouth, and shouts, "Hey you, that's mine!"

And in case there's any doubt about who that glass of water belongs to, he pulls out a gun. The deafening blast sends the barefoot women running down the corridor as the confused-looking Neanderthal drops to the ground, clutching himself and streaming with blood, and Celeste falls into the night.

14

Utterly predictable:

WORD

Keith flips the postcard over, but there's nothing else on it, no other writing, no drawing.

So that'll be the last of those cards, obviously—can't get further back than the beginning. It must mean that Celeste will be home soon.

About time. And wait till she sees what a shambles the

latest renters are sure to have made of her apartment. Well, he'll help her get it back together.

15

Cordis is not looking good. "Eat," he tells her. "I'll go out and pick something up for you, anything you like."

"Thanks," she says. "I'm fine." She looks at him with something like affection, he thinks.

He pats her soft, old cheek. "Celeste is going to be well pissed off at me when she gets back unless you start eating again," he wheedles, to no effect.

In this punishing heat, she seems to be shaking with chills. He brings over a blanket to wrap around her before he goes out with Moppet.

"Mind if I check my e-mail?" he asks when he and Moppet return, but of course Cordis never minds.

Spam spam spam spam spam spam spam. He's just about to sign out, and there it is! What he's almost forgotten he's been waiting for all this time.

It's from—not exactly his father, but close enough. It's from Kelly, the current wife:

> Hi Keith, you can crawl out of whatever hole you're cowering in, all is forgiven ☺ your fathers calmed down and called off the dogs. Mainly we want to sell

the apt so would you please come by and pick up all
those stinking sneakers and your other crap or should
I through it all out because the RE people have to
stage and they say that your sty could knock at least
1.5 off the price.

He stares at the message for a moment.

16

Kelly is trying, with one hand, to zip up her dress, a ridiculous long sparkly thing, as she opens the door with the other.
It's been a while since he's seen her, and she seems abruptly
an entirely different age than she was a second ago, before the
door opened. She'll be way over thirty by now in fact—too
old for his father. Time for a trade-in, probably.

Too old for his father, but just about the right age for
him, yum. Except for the dress, she looks better than ever.

"Can I help you out with that?" he says as she struggles
with the zipper.

"Nooooo-oo?" she says, as if he'd just said history's stu-
pidest thing.

But she doesn't protest when he pivots her around by the
shoulders and pulls up the zipper. "There you go," he says.
Right—there he goes.

She smiles, and pats her hair. "What do you think? I'm
considering this for some damn children's foundation thing
this week that your dad sprang on me. I've worn everything
I've got."

He stands back to survey her. "You look fantastic," he says truthfully.

She looks fantastic, even though the dress looks like a migraine. What could it cost, with all that sparkly shit on it? Probably more than he owes his father. Ten thousand dollars is not even latte money around here.

So he's been summoned back. How tired he is! How much he's been through! He walks past Kelly into the huge living room to gaze out at the panoramic view of the city.

"Hey," she says.

"It's okay—I'm just here to pick up that stuff," he says.

Up here, in his father's serene realm, you can't even hear the sirens. "Listen, Dad knows I'm going to pay him back— he believes me, right?"

"Nobody believes you. Ten thousand dollars? Where are you going to come up with that?"

There's no call for her to talk to him this way. And whether she knows it or not, she's basically on probation. "That's my business, wouldn't you agree?" he says.

"Oh, come on now," Kelly says. She giggles uneasily. "Hey, you've gotten taller, haven't you? Sure, Rick knows that you *want* to pay it back. Well, that you intend to pay it back. He's tired. Your old man's an old man now. He wants you to be happy, he wants you to be strong and okay. Rick loves you, you know that. Why else would he have made sure your mother couldn't get her hands on you?"

His mother wafts between them, her sweet faded gold, her sweet soft arms, musical voice, distant now, with its faint gold shine . . .

Kelly shakes her head, as if at some sorrow beyond words. "Somehow you're his only kid. Anyhow, that's what he says."

Poor Kelly—any moment she's going to be in his mother's shoes herself, along with Patti and Georgiana.

"Listen, Kelly, tell him—"

"What?"

"Oh, never mind, actually."

He doesn't need an intermediary. He doesn't need anyone. He'll call his father, like a man, and say what he has to say. He's ready to go to law school, or to business school if need be, right away. Whichever his father thinks best.

17

His head is clearing, up here—the white carpets, the clean architectural lines . . . And fortunately his dad seems to have dropped that idea about moving. But no wonder he'd been pissed off! What stupid thing had Keith been trying to prove?

Home. Yes, he's home . . . He opens up one of the craft beers that Kelly has laid in for him and flops himself out on the sofa. The noisy, confused dream of the past months is dissipating; though it has left, he observes an unpleasant stain in his mind, the residue of a disturbing dream.

What sort of strange delusion had he gotten tangled up in? It was as if he'd glimpsed himself as a different Keith—two different Keiths, ten, an infinite number, as if Celeste had refracted him through a three-way mirror . . . where glimpses of her now linger.

And she hasn't even bothered to let him know when she's

returning! Celeste! He instructs his mind to wrench her out from the reflections, from remote regions of his mind, to gather her up and consolidate her—and then to release her to dissipate in the pure, climate-controlled air of his dad's apartment.

And fold up that mirror now, please. Okay.

For a moment, a leaden, melancholy boredom seizes him

Ah, well, anyhow, no more pranks for him. Just a few more years of school, and then— He surveys the supplicant city so far below.

His sleek new phone rests on the coffee table. He reaches for it and fiddles with it idly. What should he have it do? Not much it can't.

Oh, here's a thought—"Call Tish," he orders Jeannie, who lives inside it, and Jeannie responds obediently, in that bland, untroubled voice. "Calling Tish for you."

Won't Tish be amazed to hear from him!

———

Even though he's on the other side of town now and it's not easy for him to check up on Cordis, he isn't neglecting his responsibilities in that quarter. Of course he won't take a salary from her any longer, but he stopped by just yesterday to see how she was doing and bring her a bottle of the vodka he knows she likes.

She really didn't look great, he has to say. He'll go back in a week or so to make sure she's okay, but when he left, he knocked on the door of Celeste's apartment and instructed the kids who are currently staying there to look in on her in the meantime.

"Yes, sir!" one of them said. Had the kid snickered? Keith looked at him sharply, but his face was expressionless.

"By the way," Keith said. "Have you heard when Celeste is coming back?"

The kid stared at him, and he felt himself blush.

"Celeste," he said. "The tenant?"

A group of girls seemed to be lounging on Celeste's bed in a heap of clothing and, possibly, food. "Don't worry, mister," one of them said. "Everything's under control."

Mister! The girl, though heavily made up, looked like she was about fourteen.

But to his surprise, there had been one more postcard waiting for him at Cordis's, written in some nasty-looking reddish brown ink.

it said, in letters that rippled like flame.

Pure drama, that Celeste. He shook his head, fondly after all. Well, anyhow, evidently she'll be back soon. And as he attached Moppet's leash—because since he was there, why not perform this little act of kindness—he smiled up at poor old Cordis, thinking how unlikely it was, the way this had all worked out. "Weird, huh," he said. And Cordis smiled gently back, as if she understood exactly.

18

It's not impossible that Ernst is alive, Cordis thinks, but it is impossible that he has become old himself. There he is at the site, sweating in the heat, pausing as he digs to grin at her and wave, shielding his eyes from the sun before he goes down, down, down—city beneath city, beneath city, beneath city—past the gigantic stone forms, the oldest mud dwellings, down to the early savannahs where the animal with the big brain first made its appearance, the big-brained animal so stupid—as her darling never failed to point out—that it's burning down its own home, along with everyone else's.

But it was never possible to know when he was really serious. And certainly, if she didn't have words to use, how could she have borne his absence? It's as if she's moving across a vast meadow. The fierce summer heat is spent now. Veils of gold light drift through the intense blue of the sky, and there's an inebriating scent of apples. For a moment, a bee hovers lazily, then is gone. A few leaves are already beginning to turn. A leaf detaches from its branch and flutters toward the grass. *Leaf,* she thinks, arresting it in midair, where she contemplates it. *Leaf,* she thinks, and lets it fall.

The Third Tower

Therese

Julia found it in a pile of old stuff. She didn't want it, so she said she would give it to Therese.

What was she supposed to do with that? Therese said— a beaten up old book with nothing in it but blank paper.

Well, you like to do handwriting, Julia said.

Therese looked at the thing her friend was holding. Then she reached for it.

Julia laughed and her black curls bounced.

———

That night, Therese puts it away, under her socks—her dear, neatly folded socks. And the next night when she remembers and takes it out, it seems she has come to love it in her sleep, and through the long day at work. Maybe she'll even take it with her on her trip.

It looks like an ancient thing, with its soft red cover. It looks like it has some tales to tell, hidden in those blank pages. She runs her fingers over the thick, rough paper, as if to awaken it . . .

Train

Back in the day, railroad tracks crisscrossed the entire country and trains sped morning and night to every corner of the great expanse.

That's what Therese has heard. She thinks she's heard that. Or maybe it's a scrap from a dream—or maybe it's just an error of her brain; maybe there were no trains at all.

Who knows. But what's sure is there's one train now— and it goes through the town where she lives, all the way to the City, where the hospital complex is—lucky!

Felix has hired a temp to cover for her. He's promised to keep her on when she gets back, one way or another. She's a good little worker, he says. But for now the spells have gotten so bad, they're slowing her down.

When he arranged for her to go for the cure he looked sad, she told Julia.

Hm, Julia had said noncommittally.

And it's true that Felix always has the same expression— pretty much all the old people do—of vague helplessness, as though they've just entered a day full of the troubles they've spent the night dreaming about.

But in any case, Therese is going to see the City!

Of course, they've all seen it a million times in movies

and magazines—the brilliant air, the glistening towers and monuments, sailboats gliding from the serene harbor out toward the endless horizon—the gorgeous, gorgeously dressed men and women, the broad white boulevards, banks of flowers, grand restaurants, magnificent shop windows—great, heavy strands of gems twinkling away on velvet . . .

None of the girls from housing has ever gotten to go there until now, and the others are all jealous.

Really? Therese asks; do they want to go pitching over at random moments like she does? She'd trade any day. (Though maybe she wouldn't, actually.)

But she'll be their eyes and ears, she promises.

———

The seats are so comfortable, even here in community class. There's a slight, thrilling jolt, and her heart lifts as the wheels begin to purr against the tracks.

This morning Julia knocked on the door of her room and gave her a cardboard box containing a sandwich and an apple so she won't go hungry on the trip.

Actually, she's already hungry, even though she's just settled onto the train. But she won't open the box yet.

Box! The word is shimmering and starting to glow—

Therese reaches into her satchel for her book and the pen she stole from laundry when Kyra wasn't looking—but she's too late to do whatever it was she meant to; the word has already exploded and now what's left of it is just a hard, dry little wad: box. Okay, box. She's sort of exhausted, as if she has awakened too abruptly from a profound sleep.

And then there's just darkness—a tunnel, it must be.

Now it's bright and her town is gone!

She plays a brand-new game on the seat screen, featuring zooming blobs that look like candy. Glossy! You shoot the blobs, and if you hit one just right, it emits a shower of gold coins, and then new blobs zoom in to try to eat the coins before you shoot them, too.

The rays of the sun slant at the sooty windows, moving this way and that as the train crosses over a shining river of thick, rainbow-colored mud.

But where on earth are they? Therese has never seen places like this in movies or magazine pictures—these towns! Where no person is to be seen, where the windows are broken or covered over with boards and plastic, everywhere heaps of rusted, rotted trash, with here and there a chair leg or part of an antiquated vehicle or a torn, filthy doll, sticking up from it . . .

The desolation spreads out and out, as if someone had tipped over a colossal container of wreckage by mistake. A tiny train moves through it, carrying a miniscule speck called Therese.

The train clacks slowly over another bridge—a rickety little thing spanning a cleft in the earth—and stirs up a swarm of children, who run along below, trying to keep up. Their faces are streaked with paint, or dirt. They scamper and tumble like wicked little demons, but the rocks and bottles they throw just bounce off the train's metal shell, and zoom—now they're just tiny, squiggling specks, themselves.

It's cold, Therese realizes. And her speck self is speeding

farther and farther from her friends . . . She holds the box Julia gave her tightly and looks around at the other passengers, but they're inseparably focused on their screens or devices and their faces are closed.

The sights stream by out the window, wavering, not quite solid, like pictures unfurling on a bolt of printed silk. Now there are woods. And raked-over fires, it looks like. More trash . . . an old boot? A ragged shirt . . .

A few weeks ago at supper one of the girls said she'd heard that a bunch of criminals had escaped from the prison complexes. Could Therese be traveling through that part of the country?

Fugitives—the word erupts from its casing, flaring up like a rocket, fanning out, fracturing the air into prisms and splintered mirror. Therese snatches up her book and pen and rapidly writes something down.

She's sweating. She closes her eyes and takes a few deep breaths before she looks at what the book says: *Uniforms— teams, prisoners and guards, shouting, clanging—blood and weapons. Two civil guards stumbling through trees, they trip on twisted roots, they carry a heavy pole, one of the guards at each end, a man hangs from it, roped to it by bleeding wrists and ankles . . .*

She stares at the words in the book. Horrible!

A good thing she's heading toward the hospital—maybe the excitement of travel is bad for her.

She glances out the window and takes a few more deep breaths.

No, she's okay—the glass-dust is settling, and the air is coming back together . . .

Good, the woods are behind them now.

Oh, funny! The pen has a tag on it that says, Return To Laundry.

She watches a whole series of cartoons about a cheerful creature they call a platypus. And anyhow, her town is normal—a normal, busy town. The malls are filled with people shopping.

Besides, those men in the woods—that was just a picture.

The sandwich and apple are eaten, and they have arrived. Therese brushes some crumbs off the empty box, folds it flat, and tucks it into her satchel along with her good dress—she's brought her good dress!—and her book, of course.

Doctor

Patient T716-05: Female, 17 yrs., 8 mo's. Worker, intelligence average, height/weight/appearance ditto. Word-stabilization reflex far below average. Mental "crowding" or "smearing," excess liquidity of intellection. Fainting occasional but rare. Complaint suggests aberrant cortical activity, diagnosis as yet uncertain. It is to be hoped that a course of repetition modification in conjunction with indicated elaboration-suppressants ("fuzz-offs," as the kids call them) can be devised to alleviate symptoms.

Assessment

Tree, the doctor says.

Therese looks at him, but he's studying the ridiculous-looking contraption she's hooked up to. Tree please, he says.

She thinks for a moment. Leaf, she says.

The doctor, watching some dials, frowns. Apparently the dials have registered a lack of conviction in her answer.

She tries again: Shade.

Just whatever comes to mind, the doctor says.

Trunk? Therese says.

Trunk? The doctor says.

He sighs and takes off his goggles. It's important for you to say exactly what's in your mind, Therese, not what you think I want you to say. If I could wave a magic wand and make your symptoms disappear, I would not hesitate. Unfortunately the process is more complicated than that, and we need your full commitment. There is no "right answer." What I want to hear is your spontaneous response, the one that comes immediately to mind when I say the cue word. Deception has no place here with us, nor does shame. Any truthful response whatsoever is correct.

His smile illustrates patience and forbearance.

Or probably that's a smile. His face is basically a broad stack of thick, rather squashy-looking layers, so it's hard to tell, exactly.

All right then, he resumes: Tree.

Any truthful response whatsoever! . . . She's pretty dizzy, actually, and now the word is really taking over, glowing and shimmering wildly as the air breaks up and a breeze sends light and shadows tumbling through the garden. Inside the old-fashioned house there, a child deliberates over the instrument's keys, searching for the notes signified by graceful markings on the page. Released by the child's touch, the notes detach, wavering off the page and out the open French doors, one or two or three at a time, landing awkwardly on the leaves of the magnificent tree, where they teeter for a moment before evaporating into the diaphanous air. A delicate strain of music floats in their wake, like a fragrance.

Piano! Therese says loudly.

Excuse me? The doctor says. He peers at the dials, then thumps the machine, and frowns at the dials again. Excuse me—he turns to her. You said . . . ?

The music is evaporating now, too, leaving only a phantom imprint on her senses, like the warm imprint left on a sheet by a sleeper recently arisen.

Piano—was that your response, Therese? The doctor's voice paints rough black streaks over what's left of the melody. Do you play the piano, Therese?

Does she play the piano? Huh? How could she *play the piano*? She's never even seen a piano, not a real one, anyhow! Oh—good-bye garden, good-bye marvelous tree, good-bye child, whoever you are . . . Up the sleeper goes, rising into the day, this particular day, which assembles around Therese into the gray, somewhat dingy consulting room, where the doctor, sitting across from her, waits for an answer.

Room

She has been assigned a room (614). It has a window, and a cot made up with sheets and a blanket, and a little table with a drawer in it where she puts her things.

Nothing extra. They explain: it's important for her to have as little *sensory stimulation* as possible.

In other words, she understands, nothing to set her off. There's no mirror, there are no curtains on the window, just metal shutters that are kept closed to shield her from the glittering sound of the City, from the sunlight, from the mysterious moon.

––––––

Her teachers said she'd grow out of it, but it's only gotten worse since school—words heating up, expanding, exploding into pictures of things, shooting off in all directions, then flaming out, leaving behind cinders and husks, a litter of tiny, empty, winged corpses, like scorched gnats or angels.

It's too bad about the shutters, though. Especially because the train arrived here through a tunnel, just the way it had departed from her town—as though the journey between tunnels was nothing more than a soap bubble—and then, in the station, she had stood on a moving strip of something or other that took her straight into the walled hospital complex. So she still hasn't had a look at the City.

For that matter, since the train arrived, she's hardly seen the sky.

Forms

They sit her at a screen, and she fills out scrolls and scrolls of forms. Hundreds of questions.

Her eyes and ears work fine. She's never broken a bone. Once at an Independence Day party in housing, there were some strawberries, and a few of the girls, including her, broke out in a rash that bled. But strawberries are her only allergy, as far as she knows.

She doesn't take any medications. No alcohol, no tobacco, no recreational drugs. Yes, she gets her periods. They're normal (she supposes.) They started about four years ago. No, she has never had a child. (Obviously. In housing? What, are they kidding, these people here? How do they think *that* sort of thing happens!)

Any family history of heart problems, as far as she knows? Cancer? Diabetes? Crohn's disease? Bright's disease? Kefauver's disease? Degenerate diseases of the spine or the nervous system? Malformations of the limbs or of other parts? Disorders of the lungs, liver, gallbladder?

On a scale of 1 to 100, how well does she cope with stress? On a scale of 1 to 100, how anxious does she feel? Is she willing to let the clinic divulge information about her to the registry? (Treatment is contingent on acceptance.) Who should they notify in case of emergency? (Yes, who? Felix? Julia? Housing?) Does she give the clinic permission to perform X sort of test, Y sort of test, Z sort of test?

Of course she does—why is she there, if not for X, Y, and Z sorts of tests?

Then initial here, please—initial here, initial here.

She waits in a room, and after a while she's led into another room to see the doctor again.

He sits at his large desk and calls up on his screen the questionnaire she spent the morning filling out. He explains that although of course he is already familiar with her answers, he wants to scroll quickly through, reviewing.

Ah, he says, yes—what does she mean, precisely, by this sensation of confusion she refers to? Would she please describe it as exactly as she can?

He swivels the screen so she can see it.

Confusion—right, that's what she herself typed in, but now the word looks stark. Like a . . . warrant. A warrant?

Just give it a try, he says.

She's very thirsty, but she's taking up so much of the busy doctor's time! If she were at work, she would ask Felix to let her pause for a drink of water, and of course he would.

You see pictures, I believe, the doctor prompts. I believe you noted that on the forms?

Sort of see, actually.

What are these pictures of?

Just normal things, she says.

But then—for an instant she sees the two sweating, stumbling guards and the man swinging from the pole between them, bleeding. Or of things that could be, she clarifies, things that could be happening. Or that could happen sometime, did happen maybe. Or maybe not. Something in the woods. Or a garden . . . just anything anywhere . . .

The doctor waits, but that's the best she can do.

And words sometimes seem . . . he reads from the form—sometimes seem like—what does it say here? Twins? He looks at her, eyebrows raised.

She feels herself blushing.

Maybe not twins, exactly, she says. It's like a word has the same word inside it, but the one inside's a lot bigger, and with better colors and more parts. And the inside word is sort of vibrating, jostling around, trying to get out of its wrapper? So there's sort of a halo. Or a floppy margin.

The doctor clears his throat.

All right, he says after a moment. And when do these episodes occur? What precipitates them?

Back home they thought it was something in the air. Particulate matter, she says, pleased with the nice sound. But the mask didn't seem to help, even when they changed me from the plant to the warehouse.

Not what causes them, he says—that's what we're here to find out. I meant, how do these episodes begin?

Well, they don't actually . . . *begin,* exactly. It's more as if they're just sort of happening . . .

Porous outline? he asks.

Porous outline? she says.

She glances back at the forms on the screen for some help, but it's just the forms the way she filled them out, with the answers she checked and a few little notes where she keyed in extra information they asked for. "Dizzy," it says. "Confusion."

And there are her initials, too, her initials on all the

forms. It's as if she's in a mirror, staring back at herself—the initials seem more real than she does.

The doctor looks down at his folded hands, waiting.

Tests

The hours at the clinic pass slowly, they do. The smells of antiseptics and filth. They have Therese ingest a dye, so they can observe its route as it slithers through the nooks and crannies of her brain. Needles draw fluids from her into tubes, nurses seal the tubes and put the sealed tubes into a special cupboard with flashing red lights. Other needles inject fluids into her. She waits in a waiting room. She waits in another waiting room.

Has she ever had hallucinations?

No, never.

But she sees pictures, she told the doctor, didn't she?

It's just sort of . . . pictures—not hallucinations! She's already said. Over and over.

They roll her into a metal cylinder that explores things beneath her skin. In other rooms, technicians monitor screens. A message is transmitted to her every five minutes: You're doing fine, the electronic voice says.

Consultation

The doctor paces as he explains. His hands are behind his back: We have not yet fully ascertained the etiology of your

affliction, nor have we been entirely successful thus far in iso-
lating the full play of its tendencies. The likelihood of a cul-
pable pathogen has almost certainly been eliminated. There
is, however, a consistent constellation of characteristics—a
profile, if you will—to which the manifestations of this
hyper-associative state can be said to conform, though I'm
happy to say that our readings indicate a low correlation with
the worrisome Malfeasance Index that is frequently one of
its most striking features.

Naturally, the overwhelming bulk of the literature on
the subject treats the syndrome—this susceptibility to irrelevant, excess, or ambiguous substance—as an imbalance of
some sort, a deficiency. It has been thought, variously, to be
hormonal in origin, to disclose a congenital flaw in circuitry,
to reflect a failure of character, to suggest a proto-psychotic
vulnerability, to indicate a degradation of autoimmune-
system defenses, to express the curse of Satan or, conversely,
to express the gift of holiness, to result from a regional diet
stripped of certain nutrients or from any of a number of vi-
ruses contracted in childhood.

We at the clinic regard it strictly as a physiological phe-
nomenon, a sort of synaptic leakage, so to speak, and thus
pristine, free of the moral stigma it otherwise often carries.

Our primary objective here, in addition to research, of
course, is to help to relieve the patient. This entails, as you
and I have discussed, a strong motivation on the patient's
part to pursue the goal of restored health, which in turn rests
on the degree of the subject's willingness to participate in his
or her own cure.

The doctor returns to his desk as he talks and shuffles through some papers.

How long do you think I'll need to stay? she asks.

He looks up, apparently surprised that she's sitting there.

Well, as I say, young lady, that depends largely on you.

Rest

It's a bit chilly, and the blanket isn't really warm enough. She wraps herself up in it. She's tired from her day of tests, and they've told her to sleep, because there will be more tomorrow, bright and early. But instead she takes her book from the drawer, where it's been sitting, next to the box that once held the sandwich and the apple, under her soft, folded satchel and her good dress.

She probably isn't supposed to have it? But they haven't said that, exactly—there's no rule. And she didn't ask. Though they did say that, for her own sake, she should try to refrain from brooding on things. Not only is it tiring, it could adversely skew the test results as well.

She opens the book, just to admire again the lovely, thick, rough-edged paper, but then the air starts to shimmer; it splinters, splashing words and pictures everywhere, all whirling and glittering.

She grabs up her pen: *wooden table dim cozy place. Funny song about mouse, hands clapping in time. Leaves dripping, fresh!—horse and buggy?? Bugy?? Blossoms, hooves. Glass mountain, meadow mountain tiny white flowers tiny yellow*

starflowers tiny pearl moon. Sailing moon, sorcerer moon, watch-
man moon. Clothes whisper stairway-window night fields moon
whispers. Marching band—shiny octopus-instruments—light
or swords? People long robes little outdoor tables little glass cups,
stars, moon . . .

The pictures flow by, sparkling, dissolving, blending in
their disorder, like the landscape outside the window of the
train, fading finally.

She blinks, and looks around at the stillness of the room,
the mute shutters.

She closes the book firmly and puts it back in the drawer.
Maybe these pictures are memories that somehow became
detached from other people and stray through the universe,
slipping through rips in the fabric and clinging to whatever
living beings they can, faulty beings like her . . .

She draws the blanket more tightly around herself and
snuggles into the thin pillow.

Noisy outside tonight, though. All that loud banging!

Clinic Life

They fit a metal helmet onto her, and the procedure room
darkens for a moment. Or that's what Therese thinks when
she wakes up with a dull ache in her head. In fact, they tell
her, it's hours later.

They work with her, one on one. A kind tech has been trying hard to help her with word stabilization. Did you ever

collect butterflies when you were a child, Therese? the tech asks.

Butterflies? Therese says.

With pins? the tech says. And chloroform?

———

After certain tests or procedures she's wheeled out into a darkened room. Sometimes there are a few other patients lying on gurneys, swaddled in white like her, and she comes back to herself in a sort of forest of soft groans and murmurs, faint, senseless fragments of speech.

The other day she turned out to be one of the people she was hearing. Funny! Except she was saying she wanted to go home. She hopes that didn't hurt anyone's feelings!

———

They pretty much keep the patients apart, she supposes so contact won't smudge the tests. But she begins to recognize a few of the others, just flickering past in the corner of her eye—in the corridors or a waiting room, or even sitting in the canteen. Sometimes in the woozy twilight of one of the recovery rooms.

There's a girl about her age, very thin, with chopped-off dirty-blond hair, who sends off a blizzard of quiet curses as she wakes, and a very large, very old woman, maybe fifty or so, who twists and flops on the gurney under her little sheet. Once she gets up and totters around like a big crazy giant, shrieking until she's subdued.

Therese comes face-to-face with her in a waiting room. They're both wearing the white paper robes that make them look, frankly, like lab rats. The woman looks at her with vacant, blazing eyes. *You!* she says and *you* sears a path through the air, trailing ash, before a nurse appears to lead the woman away.

Treatment

The drugs have started—she's doing better on the tests!

Tree, the doctor says.

She shuts her eyes and breathes deeply.

Take your time, the doctor says soothingly. Tree . . .

She gathers all her powers of concentration. Tree . . . she says, hesitantly.

Good! The doctor says, looking up from the dials, Excellent. He pats her shoulder. Tired? You've been working hard. His approval emboldens Therese to speak. She has been working hard, she concedes. But all that loud banging at night keeps her up sometimes.

Fireworks, the doctor explains. He smiles—she's sure of it—and she's ashamed to have complained.

National holiday season, he adds. Speaking of which, don't forget to get yourself some diversion now and again in your leisure time here—too much strain can retard the healing process. Why not take in a movie in the entertainment hall?

The Doctor Reflects

A taxing week, but one with its rewards. Patient T716-05 is showing great improvement. She's a touching little thing—limited comprehension but eager to cooperate.

It's gratifying to think of the strides she's made with the help of treatment—he's looking forward to writing this up! It was only about a month ago, after all, that her responses in the Verbal Identification tests indicated apparently almost hopeless ideation capacity. He shakes his head, recalling: "piano" for "tree!"

Any answer is valid, of course—in fact, there is a certain proportion of the population with very slight surplus-associative disorders who will respond quite spontaneously to "tree" with "leaf," or "branch." Even "bark"—even "trunk"—yes, even trunk. But such responses are considered to be within the periphery; such individuals are generally classified as "normal."

"Piano," however—clearly extrapolated from wood (itself an outer-sphere coordinate: tree > wood > piano)—is far beyond the scope of what can be regarded as healthy.

Failure to recognize the confines of words (*words, the building blocks of achievement,* to quote from his recent article on the subject in *Neural Function Today)* indicates an underlying degradation in the development and functioning of those node clusters that enable the brain to comprehend the world in which its proprietor organism finds itself, and puts that organism at risk of potentially dangerous misinterpretation of data.

What if—for example—an organism were to identify a large obstacle in front of it as (for example) the "foot" of an immense tree rather than, correctly, as the foot of a giant, prehistoric animal? Consider the possible consequences!

There is, however, a strain of current thinking in the field that categorizes those rare individuals subject to pronounced hyper-associative disorders as in some way viable: Visionaries of the Banal, as one pretentious colleague's paper on the subject styled it. (The fellow won some sort of prize for that bit of foolishness, the doctor recalls.)

In any event, it has been demonstrated that productive work can often be found for such individuals—for example, in the field of branding.

The doctor, alone in his office, chuckles (somewhat self-consciously) at the thought of a former patient, whose bizarre (though, fortunately, curable) conviction that thousands of people were being shot as they returned to their homes at night and stood fiddling with their keys at their doors turned out to be linked to his extraordinary (and ultimately very well remunerated) ability to think up names for paint colors.

(Giant prehistoric animal possibly poor example, unconvincing, revise? Haha, maybe he should take a couple of those fuzz-offs himself!)

Sunday

Therese wakes just before dawn, gasping for breath in the gray, glass-dust mist between sleeping and waking, surrounded by a static of phantoms. Can she capture some of them in her book? She starts to open the drawer where it is, but the whispering and flimmering is already winking out around her.

Just as well. She has been making high scores on the tests; she daren't risk a relapse. She closes the drawer firmly and walks back and forth in her room to shake off the phantom remnants.

The noise of the night's fireworks is still in her ears. The moon is there or not there, behind the metal shutters.

They've *strongly suggested* that she rest today. And that's just what she plans to do. She's calm enough now to fall back asleep, she thinks, and when she wakes up in the true day, she'll be careful to take it easy. Maybe just lie around and play some games.

She still hasn't seen any of the City, though—what will she tell her friends at home?

Oh, but she knows how it looks out there, they all know how it looks, beyond the hospital complex, out on the broad avenues . . .

The pealing of the bells comes faintly through the metal shutters, and when she closes her eyes she sees the sun shining, shining, the air all gold, and gold reflecting over the entire, glorious city from the Tower at its summit.

Streams of people, their arms laden with aromatic leaves and sprays of flowers, are coming from all the great houses and towers; processions pour through the boulevards to worship. The women are so beautiful—their wrists flash with jewels, and their legs gleam. Their long, pale hair flows down their backs.

At home her friends bow their heads and kneel. Julia has put a pretty Sunday ribbon in her black curls. Therese thinks: We are grateful.

Later today the others will take their weekly salaries to the mall, as they do every Sunday. Earrings, nail polish, maybe a new game, a T-shirt, a treat . . . What would she get if she could be with them?

Tomorrow a new week will begin, with more tests. And they say they'll be able to measure exactly how well the drugs are working.

Therese opens the drawer in her table and surveys the tidy stack of her possessions. She tucks her book away on the bottom.

A little dry crumb clings to the cardboard box. Do her friends at home still remember her?

She unfolds her good dress, smoothing the soft fabric and admiring the sweet flowers printed on it. She puts it on and lies down again, falling toward sleep.

Yes, she can hear the doctor's voice. Tree, he says.

Tree, she says, and a peaceful sensation radiates through her, as the word locks down.

But then for a moment she feels her unruly heart, her skin, her neurons—the secret language of her body—sending evidence of treachery to the sensors and dials. All around her, behind the wall of locked words, hums the vast, intractable, concealed conversation.

Coin, the doctor says.

She closes her ears and strains to shut out the noise.

Coin, she says. Tears of effort cloud her eyes.

Good, says the doctor. Mirror. His voice is growing softer and more insistent.

Mirror, she says—and her voice, too, is low and urgent.

Tower, the doctor says.

She takes a deep breath. Tower.

Fireworks, the doctor says.

In her sleep she struggles to scream, but she cannot make a sound.

Let's try that one again, please, the doctor says: fireworks.

Fireworks, she says.

Moon, the doctor says . . .

Recalculating

"Who is that?" Adam asked, pointing at a boy on a swing set. Adam was helping, pasting photographs into an album at the kitchen table. His mother, rolling out a piecrust at the counter, paused to look.

"That's Uncle Tommy," she said. "Don't you get flour on that."

Next there were some grown-ups sitting on Gramma and Grampa's couch. Next a lot of people in front of extra-tall corn, kids in front. "Is this Aunt Rosalie?"

"That's Rosalie all right—look at the hair."

"Are you there?"

His mother peered over at the snapshot he was studying. "That's me. The smallest one, over on the end there, with the smocked dress and the pigtails."

Adam considered the sad-looking little girl. He would have liked to pat the girl's head, but now she was just a bitsy kernel inside his mother. "Smocked dress. Smocked dress," he said, stacking the sounds up like the wooden blocks he used to play with. The tallest of the children was blurry. He must have moved. "Who is that boy, at the other end?"

"Let me—oh. That's Phillip."

"Phillip?"

"The oldest. Your Uncle Phillip."

"Oh . . ." Adam studied the picture and reviewed the jungle of legs he'd clambered about in at the last family occasion, belonging to cousins and aunts and uncles and second cousins and great-aunts and great-uncles. "He was at Gramma and Grampa's house on Easter?"

"You've never met him. He's far away."

"Is he older than Uncle Tommy?"

"Yes."

"Is he older than Uncle Frank?"

"What did I say, Adam? Phillip's the oldest. Are you going to put that into the album, or are you going to wear it out looking at it?"

Adam bent obediently over his task for a moment. "What was Uncle Phillip like when he was my age?

"I wouldn't know," his mother said. "I wasn't born yet."

"But . . . what was he like after you were born?"

She could tell Adam about Uncle Tommy when he was little if he wanted to know, she said, or about Uncle Frank or Aunt Rosalie or Aunt Hazel or Uncle Roy. But given the difference in their ages, she and her brother Phillip might as well have grown up in different households. She rotated the piecrust a severe quarter turn and bore down on it with the rolling pin. "He went away east to college, and he never came back, except once, when I was twelve, to visit. Daddy—Grandfather Jack—had expected him to take over the farm. Grandfather Jack was heartbroken. He never got over it, even though the rest of us stayed."

"Oh. Did Grampa Jack yell at Uncle Phillip?"

"Grandfather Jack loved Phillip. We all did. Phillip was the oldest. Phillip was family."

"Oh. Did he die?"

"Did who die? Of course not. What kind of question is that? He went away to live."

"Oh."

Adam kept his trusting gaze trained on his mother, while cautiously attempting, as if he were groping his way along a wall behind him, to locate a door. "Where did Uncle Phillip go away to live?" he said, with cagey nonchalance. "Did he go away to live in Des Moines?"

His mother frowned at her piecrust, now a near-perfect circle. "If Phillip lived in Des Moines, he would come to Easter. And Thanksgiving and Christmas. Phillip went to Europe."

"Europe?"

"You know what Europe is, Adam. It's across the ocean. It's a continent, like America. We'll look on the globe later."

"Was Uncle Phillip a nice boy?"

"Nice? Well, generous, I suppose. Impractical." He'd brought her a present, a sweater from France. But it hadn't gone with any of her clothes, and she had never worn it.

"What—"Adam began. His mother swiveled around to him, terrifyingly, but then blinked and turned back to her piecrust. "He never did have his feet on the ground." Grandmother Alice gave that thing away to someone who could use it. She would have outgrown it soon enough, anyway.

The pie was cooling on the ledge. The photographs were pasted carefully onto heavy pages. Adam wandered off into the newly harvested field and stretched out on his back, staring into the shining blue.

So, he had been waiting and waiting, and *finally*, one interesting thing had happened in his life—he had discovered a secret person. A person who had just slipped right out of the family pictures. The other boys and girls, who got caught by the pictures, had been turned into his mother and uncles and aunts, but his new Uncle Phillip was far away, beyond the ocean.

He sat up too quickly and closed his eyes to steady himself. Red suns flared across the darkness, and when he opened his eyes again, there was the combine, tiny, shearing off the billowing gold in the next field. The little toy figure driving was probably Uncle Frank.

Just past the combine was the curve of Adam's great planet, Earth. It was a known fact that Earth was round and that it was spinning in the middle of the sky.

God had created Earth with its vast oceans, which Adam had seen pictures of, and its blue air. But all that spinning of Earth's was what created the tides and the winds, and it was what created time, too.

Miss Brewer had explained. Earth was never still. It twirled like a lollipop on a stick, so that you looked at the sun and then you looked at the moon, and that was a day. But the lollipop was also swinging in a great, oval loop, like the rim of a platter, around the sun. It always went back right where it had started, but only when one whole year had been pushed out into space for good.

It made you dizzy to think of. Some people might be awake now on the other side of the planet, walking around in dark, upside-down Australia, and yet they would snap back onto Earth with every step they took, as if their feet were magnets. Because the real situation was, the world had no top or bottom, and he was just as upside down, right now in broad daylight, as those people in nighttime Australia were.

Miss Brewer had told them that they would never fall off Earth. But what if Miss Brewer was mistaken, and something went wrong? What if one of Earth's parts got broken, the brakes, for example, and Earth started to spin faster—*then* would they all go flying off? Would the oceans spill all over the place? Would the continent America bump into the continent Europe? Would day and night just be little strips— light dark light dark?

In fact, the wind was picking up this very instant. That was normal, of course . . . But oh—there went the stick of gum he was just about to unwrap!

Probably no one else was paying much attention, and he was the first to notice. Should he run inside and tell his mother? She would laugh at him, or say he was lying. And anyway, it was too late to do a thing about it—the blue above him was already deeper, more intense than it had been moments ago . . .

Adam clung to some bits of stubble and closed his eyes.

Hang on, he thought, as the Earth gained speed and spun recklessly into night—*hang on, hang on, hang on!*

The cause of death was given as pneumonia. There was to be a memorial in London for people who had known and loved Phillip, but the funeral was back home, strictly for the nearest of kin, who for decades had seen him only in clippings sent by a vigilant cousin living in California. When he arrived in person, the coffin was, of course, already sealed. In his absence, over time, he had brought a certain amount of honor to the tiny town where he'd grown up, and he had become a source of pride by virtue of being admired elsewhere.

Phillip's friend Vivian knew a bit about his parents, and she had written to them, urging them with just the right degree of warmth to come over for the memorial. They declined, saying that they were in poor health and couldn't travel. But it seemed that there was one relative who was planning to attend—some nephew of Phillip's named Adam, who had written her a brief note to say as much.

Squashed into his seat, streaming through the wonderful clouds for the first time in his life, Adam recalled his childhood attempts to commune telepathically with his mysterious uncle, a hazy figure, radiant and beckoning, who saw the best in him, even when others shook their heads and sighed. Too bad he had never actually dared to write a letter . . .

Day streamed toward the airplane, the plane glided downward, Adam was fitted into flowing channels of people, a train collected then deposited him—improbable as it was—only a few blocks from his destination in a place called Chalk Farm, though it was actually part of London and not a farm at all. The couple—Indian, Adam conjectured—who ran the peculiar little hotel managed to scare up an iron, and he was able to reconstitute the shirt that his pack had turned into a wad.

And a good thing, too—he hadn't anticipated the elegance of the occasion, he realized as he ascended the wide front steps of the hall where the memorial was to be held. He hadn't anticipated anything. It was the end of May. He had just finished college, and his girlfriend had just broken up with him, as well, erasing quite a lot of his envisioned future. His graduate program wouldn't start until fall, and the summer job he had rounded up in Cincinnati wasn't to begin for three weeks. He did not mention the memorial to his parents when he called to tell them he had saved up enough to take a trip. *Europe?* His mother said, as if she'd never heard the word.

In the lobby Adam's language floated softly around him, but refracted through the many accents, it sounded unfamiliar. In fact, the similarity between the exotic beings who had convened here and regular people seemed nominal. So many people, from so many different countries, each of whom looked so distinctive, so interesting, so supremely confident of his or her right to occupy space!

Say thank you, say it again, say excuse me, say please, say it louder, not *that* loud, say grace, don't get in the lady's way, ask for seconds it's polite, don't take so much, pay a call, bring a gift, don't overstay your welcome—no one in his family had ever had that look! No one in his family had ever looked like they had the right to be anywhere at all!

Or perhaps his Uncle Phillip had. Adam parked himself

next to a column in the corner of the lobby before going into the auditorium, just to gawk. Yes, it was as though aliens from an advanced civilization had cleverly disguised themselves as humans, in order to effect some purpose that had not yet been revealed to him.

Maybe some sort of practical joke. As he gazed around at the drifting crowd forming and re-forming into various configurations, one of the aliens detached herself and headed in his direction. "Hullo, great that you could make it, thanks so much, oh—Vivian," she said, as he glanced over his shoulder for whomever she might be addressing.

"Vivian." She pointed to herself. "You *are* Adam, aren't you? Did you just get in today? You must be knackered."

Her hair, a candidly artificial red, was chopped into a rough thatch that stood out, shocked, all around her head, though her small, pointy face seemed distantly concentrated, as though she were counting, trying to keep track of little rolling objects while she spoke.

So this was Vivian. Was she the practical joke? From the letter she'd written to his grandparents, he'd pictured his uncle's girlfriend as a very proper sort of lady with several chins, but despite the little lines around her heavily made up, tilted green eyes and a slightly worn quality, she looked like a child dressed up in her mother's chic suit and stiletto heels. A leggy child. The way she spoke was wonderful to his ears, and she wore a number of great big rings on her delicate, mobile hands.

"What," she said.

Oh—he had been staring. "How did you recognize me?" he said.

There was a little frill of a laugh. "Well, frankly, darling, it's like seeing a ghost. An old ghost. I mean, well, not old, obviously, a former—no . . . a what? A ghost of former times. Though, oh dear, I suppose all ghosts are that by definition, aren't they. Anyway, come, we'll do the rounds—people are wanting to meet you."

Evidently, some of his uncle's friends actually did want to meet him. Or at least to get a look at one of the relatives. He had been told without enthusiasm by his mother and his grandparents that he looked something like his uncle, but the people to whom Vivian was introducing him seemed to find the resemblance both startling and wonderful. The hair and eyes, several of them said—identical. Well, yes, those things of course—every single person in the family had the same shiny wheat-colored hair and gray eyes, nothing special *there* . . . In the blur of murmured condolences, it would not have done, he felt, to mention that he had never in fact encountered his uncle.

A group of people, widening and narrowing gently, like a circlet of waves ringing a small island, surrounded a man of close to, Adam estimated, fifty. Olive skin, black hair, cream-colored suit, eyes as pale as a wolf's . . . His bearing was painfully dignified, as if he were encased in a layer of some substance that inhibited his motions—shaking a hand, kissing a cheek . . . "Simon," Vivian whispered to Adam.

"Who?" Adam whispered back, leaning in toward her.

She patted his hand. "Simon," she whispered, a little more loudly.

"Ah!" Adam said. He felt himself flush, and for a moment his heart drummed.

They took seats in the auditorium, and a number of people, including Vivian, got up on the stage, one after another, to talk about his uncle or tell a story. The man named Simon introduced the event in a sentence or two but otherwise did not take part.

When his uncle died, Adam learned, building had already begun on his plans for a large museum gallery, entirely devoted to Asian and Islamic calligraphy, a passion of his. There was also a concert hall under construction, which he had ardently wished to see completed. But the project he had cared about most of all had been tabled. An experiment, apparently, very improbable sounding—a cluster of homes with turf on the roofs, and little windmill-type things, and reflectors to snare sunlight, and outlandish rigging so that water could be reused . . . interesting, of course, but—Adam realized he had been just about to think his mother's awful word, "impractical."

Four or five anecdotes diverted quiet sniffles into loud, grateful laughter. A small, unprepossessing man sang a few things—lieder, according to the program—accompanied by a piano, of a loveliness so distilled and potent that Adam felt he was being poisoned.

Several times Adam found himself with tears in his eyes—not of grief, exactly, of course, and yet he seemed to be getting slowly torn to pieces by some clawing thing. So many of these people were, as his uncle had been, people one read about—artists, journalists, scientists—people who were fashioning the world they had received into the world he would be living in. How was it possible that he was here? He had always thought of his uncle as someone he himself had more or less imagined, but perhaps that was backwards; certainly his incorporeal uncle was more vivid than he was—perhaps it was he himself who had been conjured up from a pallid vision of the future, to materialize here . . .

His mother would be sitting with his grandparents in their kitchen, talking about the television news or the vegetable garden or church or the weather or the neighbors, in somber, brief, ritualized exchanges, the seemly code of his childhood that had to serve for all sorrows, all joys, all fears. It was grotesque that his uncle's body had been shipped back there to the plains, where, in the uniform sunlight, it pleased God to monitor your soul for any fleck.

The prim, pastel-colored era that had completed his mother and ejected his uncle was long over, but in the region where all the family had grown up, it had been replaced by nothing. The exuberant 1960s were snobbishly passing it by when he was born, and now the venal 1980s were squeezing it dry. And the modest rural life there, with its piecrusts, its kind, tired waitresses in checkered uniforms, its Fourth of July parades, its rapidly abrading veneer of cheerfulness, had come to feel like something preserved in a bottle of chloroform, a piteous, amateur, over-rehearsed reenactment of an Eden that, come to think of it, might have been a little bit junky in the first place.

Everyone was filing out. "How are you getting to the house?" Vivian asked.

He looked at her.

"Clifford has a car," she said. "Come."

Clifford turned out to be a marvelously ugly, elegant old man who had spoken earlier, caustically and affectionately.

It was hard to imagine him doing anything so plebian as driving a car, and indeed, his *car* turned out to be a glossy, panther-like vehicle, driven by someone else entirely, a man in a uniform.

Adam was stowed in front, saving him from the strain of immediate new surprises. Engulfed in the purring of the motor as the magnificent city parted around the windshield, he could just hear the murmur of Vivian and Clifford conversing. At one moment his name seemed to sound in the air, but when he turned, he saw that the two in back were both looking vacantly out the windows, their hands lightly clasped on the seat between them.

The house had chandeliers that looked like they had come from a mermaid's palace. The floors were as shining as water. Huge mirrors brought the garden inside, with its cascading flowers. Adam stood at the open French doors watching the light splash through the leaves. The day, so fresh and glistening, seemed to contain every summer that had ever been and to promise more, endless more.

There were little, delicious things to eat, and large, fragile glasses of wine. Two musicians in white robes sat cross-legged on embroidered cushions, drawing out from another world a fragile, seeking cable of sound. Each note quivered for a moment in the air, dissolving, causing the walls to dissolve, dissolving the divisions between one thought and another, one feeling and another—rapture and anguish, resignation and yearning, twining together and dissolving . . .

The house lifted slightly off the ground. Adam clung to Clifford and Vivian. He wanted to say something . . . "You were friends of my uncle's for a long time," he eventually managed, and blushed at the inanity it had taken him so long to formulate.

"We've both known him—we both knew him—for around what?" Vivian turned to Clifford. "Oh, decades. Heavens—centuries, eternity. It feels like one second."

"Young people think it's some sort of accomplishment to know people for a long time," Clifford announced. "But after the initial effort, you see, the matter takes care of itself."

"It must be wonderful to have old friends, though," Adam said, just as he realized how tactless this was, and in so many ways.

Clifford's smile was the sort that concludes a dull business transaction. "Oh, you're bound to find that you'll have acquired some yourself. When you've lived long enough. You don't even have to like them, not at all! There they are, whether you want them or not. Yes, old friends are marvelous. Stick to your old friends. Old friends are best. Because the things your new friends do to you will be every bit as dreadful."

Clifford and Vivian chortled absently, and then, to Adam's surprise, Clifford enfolded Vivian in his arms. Her cheek rested against his jaunty pocket handkerchief, and the two of them stood there for a moment, swaying gently until he released her and turned away.

Vivian touched a fingertip to her eye, preventing a tear from spoiling her makeup. "Simon now, yes?" she said after a moment. "Are you up to it?"

Simon had regarded him steadily with the light, wolf's eyes that seemed to see all the privations of winter forests. "I've picked out some of Phillip's things for you," he said. "Things I thought he'd especially want you to have. But you must stop by before you leave London and choose whatever you'd fancy."

Adam emitted a clump of sound, but the weight of his uncle's absence dropped onto it, crushing out nearly all its meaning. Simon stood courteously, head inclined, until Adam had finished, then patted Adam's arm and returned to the cordoned-off world where Phillip was waiting for him, fading.

Now Adam had questions for Vivian, which he understood to be shockingly rudimentary. "Was it sudden?" he asked.

"Not sudden, but fairly rapid. We all knew something was wrong, but we didn't know what, or how serious it was. Simon's a doctor, though. I guess he pretty much knew what to expect, but he didn't talk about it. I don't know how much Phillip knew, himself."

They were at Vivian's. When Adam had told her where he was staying, she'd said, "Oh, no, darling—you can't. I mean, you can, of course, but why? I have a perfectly good spare room. You can just pretend it's a hotel and come and go as you please."

Come and go? he thought, as he put his pack down in the spare room. Why would he go anywhere? He was exactly where it turned out he wanted to be.

Her apartment, or flat, as she called it, was not far from Simon and Phillip's house, in a part of London called Notting Hill, which looked like a nursery rhyme. The flat was small and a little shabby, but everywhere you looked there were pictures or small clusters of toys or ceramic vases. The indigo night sky streamed in, trailing little moons and stars.

Two dogs snoozed on a rug, and he had nearly tripped over a cat.

While Vivian went to get sheets and towels for him, Adam examined a cluster of framed photos. A girl in a tutu, her dark hair up in a bun, floated through the air toward another dancer, who, serene in an impossible balance, stretched out his arms to receive her. How young the girl was! Her tilted eyes were nearly closed in the bliss of anticipation. And there she was again, the girl, in another picture, wearing leg warmers and a baggy sweatshirt, leaning back, an arm around— yes, that was Simon, definitely it was, and both of them were laughing goofily. And there was Simon again, alone, under a tree, looking out over a misty valley . . . There were no photos of anyone who could be his uncle.

He was amazingly tired and yet not quite sleepy. Vivian had made up the bed, and he lay there thinking of home, of the prairie, vast but incommodious, gorgeous and exhausting— the gargantuan farms looming in on his grandfather's small, old-fashioned one, the daily drama of producing food, the revolve of the seasons, unremitting and grand, disrupted by periodic cataclysms . . .

Out the window was the charming street, and beyond, the houses and gardens and distant neighborhoods. London articulated itself, on and on, and all of England, then France, Germany—a smidgen of Asia . . .

Almost every bit of the world was unknown to him; almost every bit of it—past, present, and future—lay beyond the dome of his consciousness, invisible to him and unimagined, and yet just as real as anything his imagination could encompass. A phantom horizon shot out all around him, a sparkling mist of sky and water, in which faint continents were rising. The planet turned in the sky, dotted everywhere with people and animals. Oop—there went a mastodon, lifting off Earth's surface into the clouds! There went Uncle Phillip, now someone else, and more and more and more— the stratosphere was thick with balloon-like angels . . .

A rectangle of faint city light hung in the dark air. He grasped at a wisp of music that had been winding through his dream, but it was gone. The afternoon came back to him, the faces, his uncle . . . He was in London; that was a window, hanging there. He slid into place and felt around for a switch. A lamp awoke.

Not once, he realized, since he'd boarded the plane had he thought of Carol. Did he miss her? It was only a few weeks ago that they had broken up. Only a day before, he had missed her achingly, had missed making plans with her, meeting her at the café, fixing breakfast with her. He had missed her body, her lilting voice, her copious, glossy, slippy hair.

She had loved to go to the supermarket with him, to go running, to go out to dinner. She was always full of plans and projects, agile in her reasoning, a frighteningly good mimic. She could imitate all the lawyers at the firm where she was interning, and trot them out for his entertainment. They had never spoken of marriage, but still, he pictured a white wooden house near a meadow, where the children could play . . .

The last morning they spent together had started out with sunlight and pajamas and toothpaste and coffee, smiles and kisses—and then, quite unexpectedly, while he was care- fully buttering his toast, there was a quarrel, swelling out of nothing, out of some infinitesimal mote. He wasn't sufficiently ambitious, she said; it worried her. "I mean, 'climatology,' what *is* it, exactly? Like, sometimes it rains, sometimes it doesn't? I mean, do you want to be one of those guys on TV with the hair?"

He had looked at her, uncomprehending for a minute—was she kidding, or had she never heard a word he had said? Her pretty face was closed.

It was as if someone had thrown a rock through the window with a note tied around it: Someone Else. A partner at the firm, possibly? Possibly even one of the stuffy, swaggering men she had mercilessly lampooned for him—one who, of course, *was* sufficiently ambitious.

Maybe *he* had never heard a word *she* said. He rose to his feet, flinging his piece of toast onto the plate like a losing hand of cards. Her defiant expression had told him that his guess was right, and the indistinct little house in his mind, the indistinct little children, were funneled up from their meadow and spat out into oblivion.

Two A.M., according to a clock on the little table next to the bed. He'd been asleep for a few hours, apparently. He shuffled into Vivian's living room, with an unfocused notion that he might acquire something to drink there. Vivian was lying propped up on the sofa near a coffee table, with a book open in her hands. Her cigarette glowed in the dimness, and the window reflected the changing colors of a traffic light somewhere; it seemed impossible, in this light, that she could have been reading.

He sat down in an armchair on the other side of the table, which held an ashtray, an open bottle of wine, and a wineglass, nearly empty. She glanced at him, roused herself, and came back a few seconds later with another glass.

She poured him some wine and refilled her own glass. "Cigarette?" she said.

The impulse to rebuke her silenced him for a moment.

"Oh, right," she said, "Well, sorry to break it to you, but all dancers smoke. Drink and smoke. We can't eat, and we have to do something, don't we?"

"Oh—" he said. "But I mean—"

"Well, not anymore, of course. But, still, there it is, old habits . . . Anyhow, I teach at least. I've been lucky. No serious irreme"—she interrupted herself to yawn—"emediable, pardon me, injuries. And some choreography."

She had exchanged her glamorous suit for a pair of floppy trousers and a little T-shirt. She still wore her rings.

"It meant really a lot to Simon that you were there today. I don't know how he got your family's address out of Phillip. Phillip never spoke about his family, never. But I suppose, in the end, he must have wanted one of you to come over."

The tip of the cigarette glowed again, like a breathing heart.

"No one told me," Adam said. "They never would have told me. I went home for the funeral, to my family's place, and I saw your letter lying with a heap of bills and things in my grandmother's kitchen. Just completely by chance. I don't know why it caught my eye."

"Subliminal clues," she said. "Great stuff, huh. You know, I tried to imagine it sometimes. What he came from. God! He was so perfect . . ."

"There was no place for Phillip," Adam said. It was like an

astonishing proclamation that had just been handed to him to read aloud, and he used the name as if his uncle were an equal, a friend, a child he had looked out for. "Just no place."

"Please," she said. "You're speaking to his niche!"

"I meant there, at home." Adam sighed. Was there something about him? Did all women consider him a complete idiot?

"Feeble joke, sorry . . . I asked him once or twice what it was like. I wanted, you know—I wanted to be able to picture it, to see him in his natural . . . as if that would solve something. But for him, it was just . . . it was over."

She shifted, uncomfortably, and as she lifted her head to awkwardly readjust a cushion behind her he saw her anguish, no longer restrained by the exigencies of the day. "It's been a long time since you slept, I think," he said. "You should sleep."

"Look who's talking." She shifted again, and lit a new cigarette from her old one.

"How did you meet Phillip?" he said, as if she really had been his uncle's girlfriend.

"Oh, it was just—I just met him. In a shop. And we started talking. You know." She grunted faintly, as though she were in pain. "It doesn't matter."

"Of course it matters," he said. The girl in the photo floated toward her onstage lover's arms. He split the wine remaining in the bottle between their glasses, and she made room for him as he sat down next to her on the sofa and put his hand against her forehead. She shifted again in exasperation, and he stroked her choppy hair back from her face. No fever . . .

"Oh, God!" she said. She clamped her eyes shut, and a slick of tears slid from between the lids.

Nothing seemed ever to change in the world Phillip and he had come from, he told her, putting his arms around her to calm her sudden, violent trembling. Everyone had been plunked down there on the sixth day and that was that—the past was a circle, and the future would be, too. There was only the winter death and spring rebirth, the ecstatic, shimmering summers, the harvest. Nothing broke the curve of the earth, the curve of the golden crops against the blue. Except, and it was an astonishing thing to see, through the wavering film of heat, when one of the storms appeared, marking the infinite sky.

First the air turned yellow. Yellow. And a black sort of veil dropped over it. And then the sooty yellow slowly turned a lush, rippling green. There were streaks of rose.

Then—everything went silent, silent and completely still. Except that way off in the sky, the black veil was spinning itself into a tiny, crazed, spinning black funnel, leaving the sky a clear yellow again, or green, as it twisted itself into shape after shape, skimming along toward you in the silence, like a dancer filled with God, growing larger and larger by the instant. All your senses were aroused and your whole body was alert, as though in expectation of some wonderful arrival.

The universe was poised, waiting. Then—a bird chirped nervously on a branch: a signal! Abruptly, a delicious fragrance released, and all the growing things for miles around started to tremble and rustle. The air was *chattering* and filled with the soft thumping and scampering of little animals as they began to *run*.

It was the voice, especially, that was Phillip's. Not only the timbre but also the accent, the cadences—Phillip's voice, assuming a presence in the room. She had forgotten how it felt, to be so light, to be lying in the sun . . . Concentrating fiercely, she gripped the glossy, wheat-colored hair in her fingers, and it glistened.

He had been in town, once, he was saying, in the silent moment, the moment just before the trees began to groan and sway. And there, on the street where the post office and the shops were, a little fawn had come clop clop clopping, disoriented, out of a stand of trees and then right along the sidewalk. Its hooves rang out against the concrete, striking sparks, and the distant funnel swam in the creature's great, dark, terrified eyes. An immense roar broke open the enveloping green; grainy darkness poured out, and there he was, the boy, scrambling down into the cellar of Dillard's Stationery just as the storm ripped the roofs from the houses on the next street and sucked them into the sky!

He was still, thankfully, sleeping heavily when she disentangled herself from him in the morning. She collected her rings from where they lay in a heap on the floor and got up to feed the dogs and cat; she would be able to have coffee alone in her kitchen, to bathe . . .

She had made her way during the rest of the night in flickering gradations of sleep and wakefulness through a thick loam, like fallen leaves, of discarded and forgotten sensations.

. . . The dim afternoon when Laura Empson had been cast as Giselle, and there had been nothing to do but go out and walk in the freezing drizzle. Such desolation! That cold hand that grabs your heart from time to time and squeezes.

Laura was a beautiful dancer, she'd insisted to herself,

and better suited to the role. And Laura was much older, Laura was twenty-six; if she didn't dance the part now, she probably never would. And she deserved the role. Lovely Laura. Spot-on for that silly git, Giselle. And besides, there were roles that Vivian was suited for that Laura wasn't. There was plenty of time for her, yet. Plenty of time . . .

There was a little jingle of bells as she opened the shop door, and he glanced up from a desk, where he was sitting with his feet up, reading. She looked away instantly, but it was indelible—the impression of the wonderful gray eyes, the broad, handsome, intelligent face, the soft white shirt.

The shop was airy and white. Silk and lace, velvet and beads and chiffon, dresses that would have been worn by lovely women long ago floated on puffy satin hangers.

She stood at a rack, moving the hangers methodically, with a tight heart, not seeing the dresses at all.

Was he looking at her? Or was he reading again . . .

She was twenty. There was plenty of time, assuming that her life were, after all, to work out. She was safely out of the corps, dancing less but dancing real roles . . . Still, so many things could happen—there were so many dangers ahead . . .

There was another little jingle from the door.

The girl entering the shop had been crying, that was clear, though the cold rain wouldn't have done much for her appearance, either. Sorrow or weather, her face was red and swollen.

This girl glanced, just as Vivian had, at the man sitting at the desk. She glanced at him and then she stood uncertainly in the middle of the room, incongruous, surrounded by the delicate, lovely, costly clothing. It was unlikely that she could afford a single thing in the whole shop any more than Vivian could.

"Hello," the man said. "Come in. Have a look around." His voice was mild, kind rather than cheerful, and he had a wonderful accent, American, but very pure.

The girl went over to a rack on the other side of the room and started moving the hangers as Vivian herself was continuing to do. She was wearing the shabbiest possible coat, an old, bedraggled fur thing of the sort that was to be found in junk shops at the time for a few pounds. The fur was hanging off, disgustingly, in chunks, as if she had been flayed.

The clicking of the hangers along the racks continued on both sides of the room, slowly and rhythmically, as if two clocks were each pedantically asserting different hypotheses.

While Vivian moved the hangers at her rack, she turned surreptitiously to watch the other fraud, who was also unable or unwilling to leave the shop. There was no doubt about it— the girl's long, scraggly hair was wet from the rain, but you could tell, from just that bit of her profile, that those were tears sliding slowly down by her ear, her large nose . . .

Vivian pivoted back to the dresses as the man closed his book and got up from his chair. He disappeared behind a curtain and returned with a little bottle of something. "Hold still, darling," he said to the girl, and she did.

Vivian dropped her pretense of inspecting the clothing and simply watched as the man patiently, moving from one side of the coat to the other, from the top to the bottom, glued patches of peeling fur back onto it. The girl wearing it stood stock-still. It was all taking a great deal of time.

"There you go, dear," the man said, straightening up and patting the coat with the girl in it. "Back in business."

For a moment the girl didn't move, but then she . . . revolved, actually, just turned on one foot and absolutely melted into the man's arms, sobbing loudly.

How small the bulky girl looked in his arms! While Vivian watched, the man held her, stroking the dreadful fur, stroking the ratty hair, making comforting sounds—just like a *veterinarian*—until the girl abruptly took control of herself, sniffed wretchedly, wiped her streaming nose on her abused sleeve, and exited without a word. The man returned to his desk and his book without a glance Vivian's way.

"Excuse me," Vivian said after a minute, and he looked up. Her voice was hoarse. "If I cry, can I get a hug, too?"

It had been pure luck; the shop wasn't his—he had just been minding it that afternoon for a friend. They spent the evening together and then the next day, a Sunday, inside by a fire, though it was only September. Out the window, the air was dark gray and vaporous; the light came up from the earth, reflected by the yellow leaves, the rain-gleaming pavement.

He loved dance, as it turned out, and became a privileged fixture at performances. Now and again he would lounge in the dressing room after a performance and watch in the mirror as she stripped off her sylph's mask and replaced it with a little light street makeup. His presence was calming and festive. They were all mad for him—the company, the musicians, the director, the choreographers . . . It was as if they had all always found Vivian special.

His work was demanding—he was already beginning to be known. Sometimes he would disappear into it for weeks at a time. And sometimes he would just disappear.

She was dancing radiantly in those days; her body was pure sunlight. They made each other laugh until they reeled like drunks, they walked around the city together at all hours, they lay tangled in her bed with music at top volume, the world swam below them like a plain, as if they had just scaled a mountain.

But he never pretended that they could stay together. When someone tells you that he'll always love you, she'd thought back then, it means he just never loved you enough.

But the 23 percent of him that was heterosexual, he said, had loved her passionately and exclusively. *Love, passion, exclusive* . . . Just words; crack them open and they were empty.

For some time she had evaded Simon, beautiful Simon, who also loved dance, who also loved to watch her, admire her, who perhaps even envied her. So she invited her two in-dispensable friends to the dress rehearsal of an austere, rather short, superbly effective piece, in which she had the starring role. Afterward the three of them went for champagne and oysters. She had left off any makeup at all, as if to be invisible while she watched the spectacle that was certain to begin in moments.

She had never remotely expected to be able to take up with Phillip again. After a time, she had chucked all her photos of him into a drawer, and it had been many years since she'd actually longed for him. After the commotion between the three of them, life had settled down to two and one. Eventually, she'd practically become a member of the household. Of course, she had other friends, too, and a few decent love affairs happened along that had consumed her interest for a while . . . It was sometime in there that her life as a dancer came to an end—the brutal price dancers pay for making beauty with their bodies.

Still, there was always the feeling that one would get around to being young again. And that when one was young again, life would resume the course from which it had so shockingly deviated.

She cried so rarely. That afternoon in the shop, so long ago, she had laughed instead as he rose to embrace her. But over the past few days, with the memorial looming, she kept losing herself to an undertow of tears. All yesterday she'd felt brittleness fretting her bones, youth streaming from her in galaxies of sparkly molecules . . .

As she made her coffee, fed the animals, moved quietly around the kitchen for fear of waking the boy, that sensation started up again, the one that had been plaguing her these days, of counting, counting—measuring the distance she was slowly traveling from Phillip's death, counting the hours until her next class, when the young dancers would come in, not carefree, of course, but with sorrows that might still be reversed or at least compensated for, counting the years since Phillip had left to move in with Simon, the minutes as they passed, while her little flat filled up with trinkets, toys, mementos . . .

The fourth—fourth!—speech, a heap of platitudes, flatteries, and bizarre flourishes, was building to an unsteady pinnacle of boringness. Any second now, at least, it was sure to finally topple over, and dessert could be brought out amid the rubble. But no—whole new incoherent embellishments were suddenly being encrusted on! How Phillip would have hated this whole event. How he would have laughed, she and Simon had said.

This current speaker was a professor of architecture, German. His hands were shaking slightly as he read on and on, but his voice was a placid monotone. This was no doubt the rough draft of a paper he was preparing for some academic journal. He himself had translated it, as he had modestly noted in his extensive prefatory remarks—hours and hours earlier.

Adam was at Vivian's right, head pensively inclined, eyes lowered, arms folded—an attitude of devotional attention. His life, which had turned out, apparently to his surprise, to be one of conferences and dinners more or less of this sort, must have given him plenty of opportunity to perfect these stealth naps.

Across the table, Adam's adorable wife, Fumiko, was surreptitiously playing with her napkin, and next to her Simon was turned slightly toward the speaker with imperturbable courtesy, eyebrows slightly raised.

As opaque as ever, Simon. What was he really thinking about? About Phillip? About the hospital or his patients or his students? About a rendezvous? One *couldn't* think about what the professor was saying—it was impossible to know what on earth it *was*. The professor had little tears in his eyes now. Either he was deeply moved by his speech, or he himself was thinking of something else.

Vivian willed a volley of darts Simon's way, and he turned, carefully, to glance at her. Age had treated him well. The lucky bastard was just as attractive—and as casually vain—at past seventy as he had been twenty years earlier! She crossed her eyes and stuck out her tongue so quickly that anyone who happened to look her way would think it was a hallucination. Simon turned back to the speaker with his almost insultingly decorous expression. Oh, that look must drive his colleagues mad!

Truly, she had never expected these plans of Phillip's to be realized, and despite Simon's façade of confidence, she doubted that he had either. Homes that supplied their own energy with sunlight and wind, that recycled their water, that returned to the earth what they took from it, and which, despite their humility, were comfortable and pleasing to live in. Phillip's least glamorous project, the most profoundly ambitious and the dearest to his heart, submerged for so many years in a swamp of bureaucracy, ridicule, and opposition, had been hauled back into the light by a firm of idealistic young acolytes.

People had already moved cautiously into the houses, no insoluble problems had yet appeared, the community was being written up in journals and in glossy magazines. The acolytes were no longer so young, and perhaps no longer so idealistic, but it had to be said that they had reason to be looking as pleased with themselves as they did, tonight. Or almost as pleased with themselves, anyway.

It had been kind of Adam to take time out of his schedule to come over. He was something of a grand presence in his field these days, it seemed, owing to a few seminal studies he had conducted concerning the environmental impact of different sorts of energy. He himself had spoken tonight, and she had been surprised by a flood of affection for this unassuming young man. Well, he was hardly young, either, of course—he was well into middle age, but he seemed like a shy younger relative, whom she was meeting for the first time since his childhood. And when he stood to make his brief remarks, she was warmed by something like pride.

In fact, she had been a little unnerved about the prospect of seeing him after all this time. Of him seeing her, truth be told. Well, but what could you do. She had steeled herself to sit down at the mirror and apply her makeup dispassionately, as if she were a nurse attending to the illness of a stranger. But when the somewhat portly fellow with thinning hair and glasses, who looked nothing at all like Phillip at that age, took his seat next to her, her heart had turned over. It was the glasses. He looked so breakable.

Months earlier Simon had been asked by the event organizers to go over the guest list, and he had conscripted her. That had been a lovely evening, lolling about with Simon. They'd both pretended to be as snooty as teenagers about the prospect of this ceremonial, and when they finished their chore for the organizers they went out for a late dinner at a lively Lebanese restaurant and polished off quite a bit of wine. Eventually they'd stumbled into a taxi together, weak with laughter, their arms around each other. They saw each other so rarely these days! How to explain it? One never managed to see one's friends any longer; they all said so. It was as if time, once a broad meadow, had narrowed to a slender isthmus.

"Who was that sitting next to you?" Fumiko asked as she and Adam walked back along Piccadilly. "The daffy old lady on your left? I talked to her for a moment before dinner, but there was so much going on."

"Ah! Well. Yes, she was a good friend of my uncle's. Vivian. She used to be a dancer."

"Oh la la!"

Years ago, when his future seemed to have arrived, astonishingly, in the form of Fumiko, and the two of them had solemnly exchanged their histories, including a certain number of humiliating, ridiculous, or bizarre encounters, it was only Vivian of whom he'd been unable to speak, as if at that delicate moment he could have done some damage to the girl in the photo and the mysterious lover toward whom she floated.

"And what about the other one, on your right, the blonde in that dress?"

"Someone with money, I gathered. An enthusiast of Phillip's. According to her, anyhow, she was instrumental in getting the project off the ground."

"Well, here's to the blond lady, then. It's a fantastic thing."

"Yes, it is." Or an irreproachable thing, at least. Possibly if the principles had been widely adopted twenty-five or thirty years earlier, when his uncle had conceived of the project, excellent precedents could have been established and a certain amount of destruction avoided. But a few well-considered houses here and there were hardly going to appease the fierce sunlight and winds that had since been unleashed, or stay the torrential rains and violent floods.

"It's so beautiful here," Fumiko said. "I wish we could have brought Nell."

"So do I. Maybe next year. Spring break."

"You know there's a terrible storm at home . . ."

"She'll be all right. She doesn't get frightened."

"Don't let's go back to the hotel yet," Fumiko said. "Let's just keep walking and walking, please."

It was May, just as it was when he'd first seen it, the city in bloom, regal and fresh. Warm, too, for London.

"Oh, wait," she said, and took out her phone. "I want a picture of you right there, to send to Nell."

They were at a great iron gate, the entrance to a mysterious park. He and Vivian had walked exactly here, more than twenty years earlier, the night before he'd returned to the States, and they had also stopped. "Has this been too strange?" she'd asked.

At the time he assumed she meant was it too strange to be half her age. It had never occurred to him until a minute or so ago that she meant was it too strange to be a proxy immortal. "No," he'd said, "just strange enough." She'd laughed and quickly kissed him. "You really are very sweet, you know. Just like Phillip."

Tonight at the end of dinner he'd kissed her powdery cheek. He helped her up from her chair; she seemed to be having some problem with a knee. He had not said, *till next time,* and neither, of course, had she.

Fumiko was fiddling with her phone. "A little to your left," she said.

It would be just twilight at home. Their dignified, ethereal Nell would be comforting her pet mouse while the thunder and lightning raged above her. Almost instantly she'd receive a photo of what was just about to be the world's very latest moment—by then so long elapsed!

"Okay," Fumiko said. "Don't move."